Avalon

Alisa White

First published in Great Britain by Author Essentials

All paper used in the printing of this book has been made from wood grown in managed, sustainable forests.

ISBN13: 978-1-78003-742-4

Printed and bound in the UK
Author Essentials Ltd
4 The Courtyard
South Street
Falmer
East Sussex
BN1 9PQ

A catalogue record of this book is available from the British Library

Cover design by Jacqueline Abromeit

Avalon

Chapter 1

The city centre was bristling with life as crowds of people marched along sunlit pavements and traffic thundered along the roads. Skyscrapers rose up into the sky on all sides, blotting out some of the late summer sunshine while a thin film of smog hung heavily in the air. The sounds of the traffic and people drowned out that of a large black car as it glided to a halt and waited for the pedestrians to clear the entrance of a side road so that it could turn off the main street.

Travelling in the shadow of the buildings, Lance was staring out at the walls on either side of him. The narrow access road was just wide enough for two cars to pass. Paper littered the ground and fluttered up into the air as the car passed before settling back down again.

Turning off the road, they disappeared into the car park that was below the building they were heading to. Artificial lights provided just enough illumination for people to find their way around, and Lance was still staring out of the window as the car came to a stop. He was in no hurry to get out of this car, and hesitated as Graham opened the door, before reluctantly climbing out.

"This way, sir." Graham broke the relative silence.

Saying nothing as he looked round at him, Lance followed him away from the car and across to an insignificant-looking door. Stepping into a featureless corridor, they walked a short distance before moving through a second doorway. With Graham stepping to one side, Lance looked about him while his chauffeur closed the door behind him. Now standing in the enormous entrance foyer, Lance could see people and traffic moving by outside through the tall windows at the front of the building. Almost everything in here was chrome and glass, offering no warmth to anyone who ventured in here.

Beyond the two lifts and the staircase to Lance's left was the reception desk, where two women were perched on stools. The older of the two peered at the two men standing before her, apparently annoyed at having been disturbed. Remaining where he was, Lance watched everything that was going on around him. There was always at least one person moving around the foyer, and the two men who had been standing by the reception desk were now moving away.

Urging Lance forwards, Graham ushered him across to the desk. More than a little reluctant, he stopped and looked across at the older of the two women. Appearing to be totally engrossed in her work, she forced them to wait for a few long and agonizing moments before looking up at them. Her irritation at being disturbed was clear to see as she peered at them over the top of her thick-rimmed glasses. Terse and more than a little hostile, she asked what it was that they wanted.

Unperturbed by her manner, Graham introduced his young companion. In an instant her demeanour changed. Immediately getting up onto her feet, she was now over-zealous in her desire to welcome Lance. Now she could not do enough to help him. Keen to personally show him up to his office to ensure that he arrived safely, she stopped and stared disapprovingly at Graham when he insisted that she call up to Rick and ask him to come down instead.

Glancing across at the younger woman as this middle-aged and slightly overweight receptionist made that telephone call, Lance moved to one side of the desk. He could do nothing but wait until this other person made his way down to meet him. Long minutes passed, Lance wishing that the older woman would stop attempting to make polite conversation. He did not want to talk or discuss anything. All that he wanted was for the year that he was being forced to spend here to come to an end. All that he wanted to do was to return home and never come back.

Chapter 2

Slowly rousing from his sleep, Lance became aware of a knocking on his front door. Checking his watch for the time, he groaned as he lay back down for a moment or two. Rubbing his face and head, he reluctantly got up and unsteadily made his way along a gloomy hallway to the door. Guessing who would be waiting out in the corridor, he pulled the door open just wide enough to be able to peer out. Focusing upon the person who was standing on the other side of the door, he unfastened the security chain and let the door swing open. He was already turning away and heading towards his kitchen as the door opened.

Watching him for a few long moments, Rick stepped into the apartment and closed the front door before following Lance through to the kitchen. Having made some strong black coffee, Lance was struggling to break open some packaging so that he could take a couple of aspirin. Putting the tablets into his mouth, he grimaced as he took a mouthful of coffee so that he could force them down his throat. His head was pounding and his stomach churned as Lance reluctantly glanced across at the one person who he had not wanted to see. Rick was watching him, sounding anything but impressed with him when he spoke.

"Have you forgotten about this trip today?" he asked.

"No." Lance sounded aggressive and abrupt. "I haven't forgotten. And I don't need a lecture."

Eyeing him suspiciously, Rick sent him off to have a shower. As Lance reluctantly obeyed, Rick called the others to let them know that they were running late. Lance knew as well as the rest of them did that they could not leave him behind, despite him making it perfectly clear that he did not want to join them. None of them particularly wanted him to join them, either. They had no choice, though.

Looking about the kitchen, Rick shook his head disapprovingly. Dirty plates were piled high in the sink while countless empty beer cans were scattered over every available surface. Lance obviously did not care what Rick was now thinking. Despite Rick having claimed that the fresh air would do him good, Lance had counter-claimed that spending the day in bed would do him more good. There was no denying that the last thing Lance wanted right now was to be dragged out on this crazy team-bonding exercise. Surprisingly, though, Lance's father had agreed to it and there was nothing that any of them could now do about it. Lance had to join them.

Having showered, Lance pulled a face at his reflection in the mirror as he dried himself, then pulled on a pair of jeans and a sweatshirt. His head still felt as though it was about to explode, and it was pounding mercilessly as he stepped back out into the gloomy hallway. Rick was still waiting for him, determined to make sure that he did actually go. From the expression on his face, Lance could tell that Rick was far from impressed with him. He did not care though. So what if he had been drinking last night? So what if he had still been wearing yesterday's clothes when he was so rudely awakened this morning? It was his time, and it had nothing to do with Rick what he did during that time.

Pulling on his trainers and coat, Lance refused to heed Rick's warnings to wear something more suitable. If Rick did not like what he was wearing, then he could always leave him here and go off without him. Sighing with frustration, Rick escorted him down to the minibus that he had parked outside.

It was early in October, with Lance having been here for just over six weeks now. During that time he had succeeded in building up a reputation for drinking far too much. They had lost track of the number of times that he had arrived at work with a hangover and had been anything but fit for work. He had shown that he really did not care whether they liked him or not, and he certainly did not want to spend this day with them out on some nearby hills. He had not even wanted to come to this country in the first place. His father was the one who had forced him to come, insisting that it would do him good to see how this branch of his business operated.

Lance sank onto the front passenger seat of the minibus, wishing that the aspirin would start to clear his pounding head. Getting in behind the wheel, Rick drove over to the offices and picked up the others. They all sounded far too loud and cheerful as they climbed in, their upbeat mood grating on Lance. With everyone safely seated, the minibus lurched forwards once more. Closing his eyes, Lance fought the desire to vomit. What was he doing here? He really should be back in bed sleeping off this hangover. Why did Rick have to come round and wake him up? Why did he have to insist that Lance joined them today? He could not have made it any clearer that he had not wanted to join them, team-bonding exercise or not.

Lance did not take any notice of the journey. He really was not interested in any of this. All he could do was sit with his eyes closed as he leaned against the window and battled his nausea. Well aware of the others chatting amongst themselves, he showed no interest in their conversation. He was not interested in this place, and hated everything that was connected with this country.

He really did not want to be here, and this journey was dragging on endlessly.

Lance was as reluctant to get out of the minibus when it came to a stop as he had been to get in. With everyone waiting for him, he begrudgingly got up out of his seat and clambered out. A keen wind was blowing, funnelled between the high granite rocks that rose up on either side of the narrow road. An autumn sun shone overhead, and white clouds scudded across an otherwise clear blue sky. Shrinking into his lightweight fleece coat, Lance was not yet ready to admit that Rick had been right earlier about his choice of attire.

Rick began to lead the group up the steep and narrow road that wound its way through the gorge. Making sure that Lance was still with them, they suddenly emerged out of the top of the gorge and moved away onto the surrounding hills. Wishing that he had heeded Rick's warnings, Lance was beginning to realize that his trainers were hardly suitable footwear up here on this desolate and boggy hillside.

Huddling into his coat as he pushed his hands deep into his pockets, Lance trudged on over the hills. His eyes were firmly fixed upon the ground before him, the open landscape that surrounded them lost to him. Refusing to join in and talk to anyone, he did not want to even try to get to know these people. There was no point in getting to know anyone here. He was here for only a year, and then he could return home and never come back.

Heavy rain clouds began to roll in along the ridge of the hill. Lance did not notice. White clouds had turned black and were quickly spreading across the sky all around them. The others, however, had noticed the torrential rain that was heading straight towards them across the hillside. They had chosen this path deliberately, and had almost succeeded in reaching the outermost trees of a nearby wood before that rain reached them. Drenched, Lance was the only one who did not find this experience amusing. His mood mirrored the weather perfectly. His head was still hurting, his mouth was furry and now he was wet and cold. How could these people find so much humour in this situation that they now found themselves in?

Sheltered by the trees, the group stared out at the incessant rain. It would take at least half an hour to walk back to the minibus, and the rain was falling so heavily that they would all get soaked to the skin if they attempted to return to the vehicle just yet. Sighing, yet remaining good-humoured, the group turned their backs to the open and exposed hillside so that they could peer more deeply into the woods. Within moments they had decided to explore the place while they were sheltering there, Lance having no choice but to begrudgingly join them. He had no idea where the minibus was. Having paid no attention as they walked away from it, he was now left with no option but to join in with this stupid little game. Against his wishes, he was ushered away from the outer edge of the wood as they moved further in among the trees.

A single narrow path wound through the trees, and Rick now let one of the others lead the way. With three people in front of him, Lance appeared to be both annoyed and irritated about having Rick follow him along this track. Rick was still trying to coerce him into joining in with the conversation, but Lance remained stubbornly silent. With his eyes firmly fixed upon the path before him, he remained sullen as he tried to shut out everything that was happening around him.

Suddenly slowing a little, the person who was leading the group along the track hesitated as he called back. Ahead of them, a strange white light glowed eerily, attracting them towards the spot where it was shining. Moving on, they continued to follow the track until they suddenly and unexpectedly emerged out into a clearing. Having taken no notice of the group ahead of him, Lance was forced to come to an abrupt stop upon almost walking into the person who was directly in front of him.

Annoyed, Lance looked up and stared at the scene that was before him. Only now did he realize that they had stepped out into a large clearing. They were standing close to the bank of a large lake, its cold, still waters glowing beneath the eerie white light that was shining down on it. White mist was hovering above the water's surface, moving and shifting constantly as it exposed and then hid the green reeds that were growing up out of the water.

The white light that was illuminating the clearing made Lance appear paler than before, his eyes looking darker as he stared unblinkingly at the island that was at the centre of this lake. The mist was swirling constantly around it, changing its shape all the time so that he could not picture it in its entirety. Covered in trees, none of them could see a spot where anyone could land over there.

"Hey, let's go over there and explore it," one of the group suggested, breaking the eerie and unnatural silence that had descended upon them.

Tearing his eyes away from the island, Lance looked round sharply at the person who had made the suggestion. At the same time another voice could be heard, making the whole group look round at the nearby trees. Standing beside one of those trees, a young woman was clad in a heavy, brown, full-length dress that was covered by a green cloak. The hood of the cloak was covering her head, hiding her hair as it cast a shadow over her face.

Staring at her, Lance could not tear his eyes away. She seemed to be looking directly at him, as though hypnotizing him with some kind of spell. Her words were slowly filtering through into his mind, Lance hearing what she was saying a second or two after everyone else. They would never reach the island, she claimed, no matter how hard they tried. Many had attempted to do so, and had only succeeded in sailing straight through, as if the island had split in two before reforming again afterwards.

After a short and tense silence, everyone around Lance began to snigger. They had never heard of anything so ridiculous. It was simply not possible for a solid mass of land to move in the way that had just been suggested. With the group laughing openly at her, the young woman noted how Lance continued to gaze at her. He was not laughing; instead his features were serious as though he was actually daring to believe her.

"So if it is impossible to reach," one of the group questioned, "what is that place?"

Shifting her gaze to this other person, the young woman did not answer straightaway. Then, slowly, an unnerving and wistful smile spread across her face.

"What is that place?" she repeated, sounding genuinely surprised that they did not know.

Once again her gaze moved back to Lance, and she continued to stare at him as she answered. That island was Avalon.

Chapter 3

Lance was unable to stop himself from staring at the young woman who was standing nearby. Though he could occasionally glimpse the brown dress that was beneath her green cloak, its hood was covering her head so that he had no idea of the colour and length of her hair. Her pale skin made her eyes appear even darker than they truly were. Having never heard of Avalon, he had no idea what she was talking about.

The rest of Lance's group had become nervous, all of them now constantly glancing across to the mist-shrouded island that was at the centre of the lake. The eerie white light that continued to shine down upon it added to the unnerving atmosphere, giving the island and its lake a regal and magical aura. Despite what they could see before them, not one of the group members seemed to believe the claim that had just been made.

"Avalon does not exist," one of them eventually declared. "It's not a real place. It's just a myth."

Smiling with a quiet confidence, the young woman moved her hand from where it was resting on a tree trunk and reached inside her cloak. The loud denials from the group only succeeded in increasing their doubts. There was no need for her to utter another word. Surely it could not possibly be true? They could not possibly believe that they were looking at the fabled Avalon.

Still staring at the young woman, Lance jumped slightly when a man suddenly emerged from the trees and stopped alongside her. Wearing a short, waxed coat over his jeans and sweatshirt, he reluctantly confirmed that what the young woman had just told them was true. No-one had ever been able to land on that island, and though many people had attempted to do so, all of them had failed. He had seen with his own eyes the way that the island appeared to move in order to prevent anyone from reaching its shores. He did have his doubts that it was Avalon, though. Gwyn was known to be a fantasist, and it was best if they simply ignored her.

Having insisted that she left the group alone, he appeared annoyed when she looked back over at them, unable to stop herself from staring directly at Lance. There was the hint of a smile on her face as she held his gaze for a few long moments before reluctantly turning away. As she was ushered away through the trees (a little too keenly), her companion's harsh words rang loudly inside Lance's mind as he told Gwyn that she should have stayed away and left them alone.

Continuing to stare after Gwyn as she disappeared away through the trees, Lance was feeling confused. Her companion had labelled her a fantasist, but then he had also admitted that she had told the truth about the island that was at the centre of the lake before them. Those harsh words had given Lance the impression that she was a virtual prisoner who was to be ridiculed and humiliated at every possible opportunity.

For a few moments Lance continued to stare at the spot in the trees where she had disappeared from sight. Then he seemed to snap out of his trance and looked back across the still waters of the lake to the island. The mist that was shrouding it moved constantly, giving him the impression of a continuously changing shape. Without warning, his curiosity had been roused. There was something about this place and what had been said that left him wanting to find out more; to stay here; to embark on a journey of discovery.

The rest of the group, however, were nervous and restless as they started to head back into the trees in order to escape. Now Lance was as reluctant to leave this place as he had originally been to join the group on this outing. Now, just like that young woman had been a few moments ago, he too was being ushered away through the wood to leave this lake and island behind.

The worst of the rain had moved on by the time they emerged onto the open hillside again. Only now did they realize how sheltered they had been while in the woods. They had experienced no apparent weather conditions while among those trees. The atmosphere had been calm and serene, leaving them with a sense of an ancient time from many years gone by. The wind was blowing more strongly out here, buffeting them constantly and mercilessly as they headed back to the minibus. Hardly aware of the wind or the sporadic rain that was falling, Lance followed them across the exposed hillside. He took an interest in his surroundings this time, looking about him as they walked.

Eventually they reached the gorge, and Lance reluctantly followed as they walked past the minibus and sought shelter in a café. Sitting at a table with mugs of steaming hot coffee before them, he ignored the group's conversation, lost in his own thoughts. There was no denying that his curiosity had been roused, and those few precious words that had been spoken were now spinning round in his head. Determined to return and discover more, he could clearly remember the route across the hillside to the wood.

Still wrapped up in his own thoughts, Lance followed the others back out to the minibus when they were ready to leave. The wind was still being funnelled through the gorge, making him shiver as he looked up at the grey and black cliffs that towered above them. Being wet from the rain was beginning to make him feel numb with cold, and glad to climb back into the minibus, he sat and waited as everyone else joined him.

Checking out the route to this spot as they headed back to Bristol proved to be impossible. The incessant rain outside and the windows constantly steaming up were enough to make Lance give up, frustrated. At last they were leaving the rest of the group outside the offices before returning the minibus to the rental firm. Gazing out of the window, Lance did not notice how Rick glanced across at him as he drove. They exchanged the minibus for Rick's car, and Lance continued to remain silent until they reached his apartment block.

"What's Avalon?" he asked, absentmindedly unfastening his seatbelt as he gazed up at the building before them.

"What's Avalon?" Rick repeated, sounding surprised. "Don't you know? It's the final resting place of King Arthur. Everyone knows that. It doesn't actually exist though; it's just an old legend. Don't take any notice of that young woman – I'm sure she's harmless enough, but she obviously lives in some sort of fantasy world."

Hesitating, as though waiting for an answer, Rick added that he would see Lance in the morning, before suggesting that he did not drink any alcohol for the rest of the evening. Nodding,

Lance said nothing as he climbed out of the car. It was raining here too, making him reluctant to make his way across to the building before him. To stay here with Rick would mean more lecturing, though.

Hurrying across to the shelter of his apartment, Lance showered for the second time that day; then made some coffee and a sandwich. Curiosity was gripping him and would not let him go. Sitting down on the settee in the living room, he absentmindedly took a bite from his sandwich as he began to research Avalon and King Arthur on his laptop. Everything was quiet in the apartment as Lance continued to gaze at the screen. All too easily he had mapped out his route back to that gorge and that wood with the hills beyond it. Reading about King Arthur and his knights, he could so easily picture himself back on the shores of the lake once again. Lost in a dreamlike state, he jumped before snatching up and answering his ringing mobile phone.

"Cindy?" Lance swallowed, the information on the screen before him fading as guilt took hold. "I'm sorry; I was about to call you. We've only just got back from some team-bonding exercise."

"You've been out on what?" Cindy sounded far from happy. "Since when have you ever done anything like that?"

"It was my father's idea. He thought it would do us good. Have you got someone with you?"

Lance had gone cold. He was certain that he had heard a muffled sniggering in the background.

"Of course I haven't! How could you suggest such a thing? What are you thinking, Lance? Making me wait for hours and still not calling me, and then you accuse me of being with someone else!"

The line went dead, giving Lance no chance to react. He knew what he had heard, though, and he was now beginning to doubt his former assumption that Cindy's mother was with her. Cindy had frequently lied to him before, and now her reaction was enough to convince him that she was lying to him now, too. Sighing with frustration, he switched off his phone and put it back down on the coffee table before taking another bite from his sandwich. For once he was glad of Cindy's abruptness in ending the call. Instead of talking to her, he could continue reading more about this ancient Celtic myth.

The room fell silent again, Lance quickly becoming totally absorbed in the tale. It was so easy for him to imagine it all: the battles the knights had fought and the heroic deeds that had been performed. It was all so different to his own dreary world. Arthur's world was exciting, making him feel alive for the first time in his life.

Suddenly catching and holding his breath for a couple of moments, Lance felt his heart skip a beat. Staring unblinkingly at his screen, he read a handful of words over and over again. King Arthur's wife, his queen, was called Guinevere. Surely it could not be true. Performing another search in an attempt to gain more information, he waited impatiently as he continued to stare at his screen. It was true. Guinevere, daughter of the Scottish King Leodegrance, was the wife of the legendary King Arthur of Camelot. She had allegedly had an affair with King Arthur's chief knight, Sir Lancelot.

Swallowing, Lance browsed around the page but could find nothing but a simple sketch of Guinevere. To him, there was a clear resemblance to the young woman he had met only a few hours ago. His head was spinning; his imagination running wild. Could she really have been Guinevere herself? If it was true, he could see no reason why she should lie about the identity of the island in the lake. Who was the man who had been with her – King Arthur himself, or maybe Sir Lancelot? Unless Lance returned to the lake in the wood, he would have no way of knowing. A determination to do just that was taking hold as his fascination with this tale grew rapidly. A thirst for knowledge was quickly becoming an obsession. All sense of time was paling into insignificance. Right now, nothing else mattered.

Chapter 4

Rick's annoyance was clear to see as he rapped sharply on the door of the apartment. Lance was supposed to have been at the office over an hour ago, yet Graham had confirmed that there had been no sign of him. Over and over again Rick had asked himself how many chances his young charge needed. Son of his employer or not, he could not keep giving excuses for his behaviour.

At last Rick could hear someone moving about in the apartment behind the door. Seething with anger, he could only wait impatiently for the door to be pulled open. Then Lance was looking out at him, actually looking genuine for once as he immediately apologized. Admitting that he had not heard his alarm clock ringing, he was already heading away along the hallway when Rick stepped into the apartment.

"Lance," Rick called out, "I think it's time for us to sit down and talk. I want to know what's going on."

"I've not been drinking," Lance stated, his voice defensive and hostile.

"I never accused you of doing so," Rick pointed out, "but if it wasn't for the fact that your father owns the company, your behaviour would have easily cost you your job by now. I need to know what's going on. Is it really that awful being here with us? I can understand how hard it must be for you, being such a long way from your girlfriend —"

"You don't know anything," Lance blurted out bitterly. "I can't stand the sight of her."

Rick was completely lost for words, and there was an expression of genuine surprise on his face. His anger and indignation were gone. Lance's reaction had caught him completely off-guard. Staring back at him, Lance noted the expression on his face and sighed as he looked away again.

Rick continued to gaze at Lance. Sensing that he had jumped to conclusions, he was now feeling guilty for being irritated by Lance's behaviour. Now he realized that he knew nothing about the young man before him, who now appeared vulnerable instead of unfriendly. Softening, Rick quietly encouraged him to tell him what was going on.

Hostility could be seen in Lance's eyes when he looked back at Rick. Not understanding why he should still be so unfriendly, Rick gently urged him once more to talk to him. Lance asked him why he should care, but incensed at first, Rick's indignation quickly subsided. He had asked himself the same question on many occasions, he explained, but the fact was that Lance's behaviour since his arrival had done nothing to endear him to anyone here. If they were to work together over the rest of this year, though, Rick wanted to know the reason for the way Lance was behaving.

Lance was still glaring at him, and Rick was beginning to wonder why he had bothered to try to reach out to him. He had believed that he would be able to break through the protective shield that Lance had built up, but he was getting nowhere, and could think of nothing else to say that would remove the barrier that was repelling him. Frustration was taking hold; Rick almost giving up and turning away when Lance suddenly seemed to give in.

Minutes later, and they were sitting in the living room with mugs of coffee in their hands. Rick could see how nervous and insecure Lance now was. He was doing everything that he could to avoid Rick's gaze. Watching him, Rick noted how Lance had retreated behind his barrier again. It was not going to be easy to get anything out of him.

"Come on," Rick urged, breaking the tense silence, "tell me what's going on. How come you're seeing someone who you hate so much?"

Not reacting at first, Lance glanced across at Rick as he constantly moved his fingers around his mug. He appeared to be desperately trying to resist revealing anything, but any resolve quickly disintegrated as Rick coaxed him into speaking.

"From the moment I was born, my father has had my entire life planned out. He wanted a son to inherit his company, so when I was born that wish was fulfilled. He's made all of the decisions and all of the arrangements. He chose who raised me and what I was taught. I've never been to school. He paid someone to teach me at home, but only about his company and the computers it makes."

"What? You mean you don't know about anything else? So when you asked me what Avalon was yesterday, you weren't joking."

Losing his confidence, Lance again needed to be encouraged to continue. As he began to talk once more, Rick fell silent. Lance confessed to having researched the subject of Avalon when he arrived back here the previous evening, and he had lost all track of time, which was why he had not heard his alarm clock this morning, though he realized that it was no excuse really. Rick could sense that Lance was going to fall silent, and feeling intrigued, he encouraged him to continue.

Swallowing, Lance still refused to look at Rick. Despite all the teaching he had had as a child, he had never been able to do anything that was good enough for his father. No matter how hard he tried, his father was never satisfied. He was a disappointment, and his father constantly reminded him of that fact. He had wanted someone who was worthy of taking over his empire, but instead he had someone who would never be able to achieve what his father wanted him to achieve. Then Jim Peterson had come to his father one day —

"Jim Peterson? Not the Jim Peterson who owns Peterson Computing and Diagnostics? What did he want?"

Interrupting Lance had not been Rick's intention. He had not been able to stop himself from blurting out his obvious surprise that Blake Brookes should have had a visit from his arch-rival. He had unintentionally succeeded in getting Lance to look at him with his outburst, though. Nodding, Lance was now more than willing to explain.

Jim Peterson was Cindy's father, and he had visited Lance's father to suggest that Lance and Cindy get married. As mad as it sounded, he had suggested that the marriage could signify a union between the two companies. Having laughed at his rival at first, Lance's father quickly realized what the advantages would be. He honestly believed that he would rule over both companies one day. What he could not see was that the Petersons simply wanted to eliminate the only opposition they had, but there was no talking to Lance's father. If Rick had met him, then he would know that his father spoke and everyone else obeyed him without question.

Finding it hard to believe what he was being told, Rick could only gaze at Lance. Still not looking back at him, Lance continued talking. He had been working alongside his father every day for the last two years. His father was so disappointed with and ashamed of him, though, that he had sent him over here for a year just to get him out of the way. When he returned home, he was due to marry Cindy, but although she acted as though she was keen, she hated him as much as he hated her. She only wanted to go through with it so that she could get her hands on the company.

Then Lance fell silent, as though he had confessed everything that he needed to. Rick was lost for words. Everything was now so clear. Now he could understand why Lance appeared to be so sullen: he did not want to befriend anyone here because he would never see them again when he returned home. It appeared that he was in an impossible position; trapped in an existence that no-one should be forced to tolerate.

"I'll think of something." Rick eventually broke the uncomfortable silence. "I'll help you out."

Lance looked at Rick, a deep sadness in his eyes. No-one could help him, he claimed. There was nothing that anyone could do to put a stop to the plans that had been made. Continuing to gaze at Rick for a few moments longer, Lance suddenly got to his feet and put his mug down onto the coffee table. The barrier had gone back up again, and Lance's hostility was back with a vengeance. Not wanting to say anything more, he hurried out of the room and dressed for work.

Watching Lance, Rick could see that he was not concentrating on his work. After everything he had told him yesterday, Lance was now behaving as though nothing had happened. He was nervous and insecure again, and Rick knew that he would not be able to coax anything out of him today.

Waving his hand in front of Lance's face, Rick smiled as a flicker of life appeared in Lance's eyes. Quickly looking about him, Lance apologized as he shifted his weight on his chair in order to find a more comfortable position. Rick was far more tolerant of him since their conversation yesterday, and that made him more nervous.

Rick, meanwhile, had thought of nothing but that conversation since it had happened. He wanted to know more, and was certain that he had not been told everything. He could sense that he was going to get nothing out of Lance while here at the office, though, and keen to usher him outside for a break so that he could quiz him some more, Rick was taken by surprise when Lance refused. About to speak again in a bid to coax him out of the room, Rick looked up as the door opened. He had not taken any notice of the sound of stilettos echoing sharply and loudly on the outer office floor. The flinging open of the door announced the arrival of the owner of those stilettos, and Rick was immediately indignant at having been so rudely interrupted. This woman had not been invited in, yet in she had come as though she owned the building.

Rick stared at their visitor, his annoyance clearly showing. Her professionally styled blonde hair was cut into a short bob, and her large, bright blue eyes gazed at the pair seated at the desk. Carelessly throwing her expensive, tailor-made coat across the back of a nearby chair, she moved further into the room.

"Cindy!" Lance exclaimed, his eyes wide with shock and disbelief.

"Is that it?" she questioned, brushing her hands down her designer dress. "What kind of greeting is that for your fiancée? I've come all the way here, and that's all you can say?"

Too shocked to move, Rick could only watch as Lance apologized and grovelled embarrassingly as he offered her a chair. Moving towards the chair, Cindy stared directly at Rick as she prompted Lance to introduce her. Greeting her politely, Rick suddenly felt unimaginably uncomfortable as she looked him up and down. There was no denying how over-confident and domineering she was, and Cindy was obviously fully aware of the power that she held. Rick could feel the hairs on the back of his neck bristling uncomfortably as he offered to fetch them some coffee.

"Oh we're not going to bother with the cheap coffee that this company offers. We'll find a Starbucks; get a proper coffee there. Come on Lance. You can finish for the day now and show me around this dreary-looking town."

Desperately looking to Rick for an excuse to stay, Lance was getting no support. Rick was feeling as helpless as Lance. Cindy's whole manner demanded obedience. She was obviously used to getting exactly what she wanted, and Rick felt as though he had no choice but to let Lance go. Having told him only yesterday that he would help him, Rick could now understand why Lance had claimed that no-one could do that.

Cursing silently to himself, Rick could only watch as Lance followed Cindy out of the office. Fully aware of the lewd comments that were being made, he chose to ignore them as he called one of the men into Lance's office. Moving further into the small room, Rick brushed aside Will's apology and earlier remark. He was gazing out of the window, watching out for the moment when Cindy and Lance appeared on the street below.

"Have you heard of Jim Peterson?" Rick asked, not looking round. "He's the young lady's father. He and Blake Brookes have arranged their marriage for next summer; it's all being done so that the Petersons can get hold of this company, but if you'd met Lance's father, you'd understand that there's nothing Lance can do to put a stop to it. He's not being allowed to do anything for himself. He's trapped in a miserable existence, and I want to help him escape."

And how, Will asked, did he intend to do that? Staring out of the window, Rick watched as Cindy and Lance emerged from the building and climbed into a waiting taxi. Still not looking at Will, Rick told him that Lance believed that Cindy was seeing someone else. He needed someone to do some snooping.

Will swallowed. He knew what Rick was silently suggesting.

"Any chance of getting me a camcorder?" he asked. "And I'll need some time off work while Lance is here."

Smiling sadly, Rick patted his shoulder as he thanked him. He needed Will to succeed, otherwise Lance would be doomed. If he was going to help Lance, then this had to work.

Chapter 5

Rick's stomach was feeling uncomfortable. Checking the time yet again, he looked across at the door before glancing at Will and looking back as a movement caught his eye. Lance had arrived. He looked tired, Rick thought as he watched him hurry through the outer office to his own small office, refusing to acknowledge anyone and therefore making it impossible to tell whether he was aware of the smirking and sniggering.

Feeling annoyed with everyone's reaction, Rick got to his feet as Lance disappeared through his office door. He looked at Will and nodded just the once; then headed for that doorway. He had noticed how Will had not joined in with the comments that were being made. Maybe, if they knew the truth, these people would not look upon Lance as being lucky for having such a stunning girlfriend. Maybe then they would understand why he was always so sullen.

"You look tired," Rick remarked, closing the door behind him.

"I don't want to talk about it," Lance stated.

His response was quick and terse, and Rick was taken by surprise at Lance's abruptness. He was standing by the window and staring down at the street below, and Rick wondered how to continue. Lance sounded as if he had rebuilt his defences, his wariness suggesting that his protective shield was now stronger than before. Trying to think of something to say, Rick kept quiet as Lance suddenly continued. He had no idea why Cindy had come to see him. She had only ever treated him with complete disdain and disrespect, but yesterday had been very different. She had never shown that kind of interest in him before. Yesterday she had pestered him constantly, giving him no peace until the early hours of the morning.

"She's a very attractive lady, Lance, and she's your fiancée. Under normal circumstances, any man would jump at the chance of spending the day with her instead of being at work. Maybe you should go home and get some sleep."

"I won't get any sleep while Cindy's there," Lance snapped.

The hostility had returned, and Lance continued to stare out of the window. He did not want to discuss Cindy. Unfortunately she was not planning on returning to Boston before next Tuesday, and he did not want to take any more time off work while she was here. She was the last person he wanted to be with.

Rick swallowed, forcing himself to quell his rising indignation as he made his way across to where Lance was standing. Lance was engaged to

Cindy, and it would have been normal for him to take time off when she visited from another country. He realized that their relationship was not normal though, and he would have refused to let him go yesterday if he could. He had not been able to do that, though, no matter how much he had really wanted to. He did want to help him, really he did.

Rick fell silent as Lance glanced at him and sighed. No, their relationship really was not a normal relationship. It was anything but normal. It was completely one-sided. For him it was nothing but a nightmare; a nightmare from which he could not escape. He was prepared to do anything to find a way out and be free of Cindy, but Cindy and her mother had been busy making the arrangements for their wedding. They had decided upon a lavish ceremony in the extensive grounds of their house in the hills outside Boston, and Cindy had just announced that her father had bought her the waterfront apartment in Boston that she wanted. There was no way out for him. He was trapped, and had been trapped since the day that he had been born.

Following a brief and tense silence, Rick asked if Cindy planned to do anything while she was here. Lance shrugged his shoulders, his voice full of spite when he spoke. Did Rick mean when she eventually decided to get up? He did not doubt for a moment that she would search through all of his things in a bid to prove that he was dishonest, but she was destined to be disappointed – there weren't even any beer cans. He had disposed of them all before she had arrived unannounced.

"She likes to spend a lot of time on her laptop," Lance informed him, gazing out of the window again, "though don't ask me what she does. Whatever it is, I'm not interested. She's said that she's going to book a hotel in London for a couple of nights, so I'm fully expecting her to insist that I don't come here on Friday. She wants us to catch a train to London on Friday and come back on Sunday, and I'm not going to deny that I'd much rather do this lousy job instead."

Lance hesitated, sensing Rick's shock. Sighing, he apologized. He only hated this job because it had been forced upon him by his father, and he had not wanted to get to know anyone here because he feared missing them when he returned home. He had never found it easy to speak to people as his father had never let him socialize, but now he feared that he was getting too friendly with Rick. He had been so patient, reaching out to him instead of giving up and turning his back on him. He was acting as though he actually cared, and Lance was not used to that. For the first time in his life he felt as though he had someone who he could trust and confide in. He knew that Rick would treat everything that he had told him with the strictest confidence.

Rick was feeling guilty as he smiled sadly. He had discovered that Lance was a good lad who was trapped in an impossibly miserable situation. He could not even begin to imagine what his life must have been like. They had all misjudged him badly when they had believed that he was moody and aloof. The brutal reality was completely different to what they had imagined, and now the snide remarks that had been made when Lance had arrived this morning only made Rick angrier. If they achieved nothing else while Lance was here, Rick wanted to release him from his living nightmare.

Rick stood on Will's doorstep, nervously looking up and down the street as he waited for the door to be opened. An eternity seemed to have passed before the door was pulled open, Rick hesitating and checking the street once more before stepping inside. Will appeared shaken, and Rick jumped a little when he quickly shut the door as soon as he was in the house. They were in a dark and narrow hallway, and Will ushered him through a nearby doorway.

Will was agitated and trembling a little as he hurried past Rick. Surprised, Rick watched him for a moment before looking around the living room and perching on the armchair that was offered to him. The room looked cluttered, the minimalistic furniture more than filling the available space.

"I called Trent over in Boston last night," Rick explained, noting how Will glanced around at him while picking up a DVD, "and he confirmed everything that Lance told me. Blake Brookes has only ever been patronizing with Lance. Apparently he's found great satisfaction in belittling his son all the time. The lad's had no-one standing up for him throughout his entire life. I guessed Blake was a tyrant when I met him once, but I never suspected that he'd treat his own son in such a way."

"Well, add this to what you've already found out," Will told him, pushing the disc into his DVD player. "I'm telling you, Rick, she's a nasty piece of work. If the others knew this, they wouldn't be saying that Lance was lucky to have her. If you don't mind, I'd rather go and make some coffee than watch it again."

Curious, Rick watched Will scuttle out of the room, then looked back at the television. It would take a lot to leave Will as shaken as this. Rick had never seen him behave in this way before; he had only ever remained calm and in control during any crisis they'd faced together. Rick wanted to know what had happened to reduce someone like Will to a nervous wreck. The DVD was already playing, and Rick immediately felt threatened and vulnerable as he watched Cindy opening the door to Lance's apartment. How could a young woman make grown men react in this way?

Perching further forward on the armchair, Rick watched and listened carefully. He was not interested in Will's excuse for being there. Using a false name, he had been careful not to reveal his identity as he talked to Cindy. Unbelievably, she was eagerly and willingly confessing to so many things while desperately trying to seduce her visitor. She did not know Will, had never met him before. Yet what she was seeking from him was obvious.

"So what if I'm engaged?" she said, flirting outrageously as she did so. "I'm only marrying Lance so I can get hold of his father's company. It's the easiest way of eliminating our only rival. Once I've got that, then I can get rid of Lance. He's no use for anything else."

Rick shifted his weight in the chair, still listening intently as Will sounded shocked when reacting to her comments. Surely her fiancé was not that bad? Cindy's harsh laughter grated on Rick's nerves. She could see nothing worth looking at when looking at Lance. He was nothing but a great disappointment to his father. He would never achieve anything in life. He lacked drive and ambition, and was nothing but his father's puppet.

Cindy was talking freely, boasting openly to this complete stranger. Blake Brookes was someone who she could never respect. She had never met anyone who was so stupid and arrogant. He believed everything that she told him, no matter how ridiculous. He had not deserved to succeed in the way that he had. He belonged in the gutter, alongside all of the other ignorant and obnoxious people.

Rick involuntarily moved back in the chair as Cindy moved towards the camera. Immediately feeling vulnerable again, Rick swallowed as he cursed under his breath. Cindy had only lunged across to Will, and was now rubbing herself against him. She had no idea that he had a concealed camera with him, recording everything she said and everything she did.

"Sorry ma'am." Will was pushing her back. "You're a very attractive lady, but you're also spoken for. I don't want any accidents."

"You don't want to get me pregnant, you mean?" Cindy smirked, unperturbed. "Oh, there's no chance of that, seeing as I am already. It's not Lance's, before you ask. He's not capable of doing something like that. My parents have told me to come here and do whatever is necessary to convince him that he is the father, and unpleasant as it is, that's exactly what I'm doing here. I have to, so we can get hold of that company. He's that useless, though, that he's left me feeling very frustrated. What I need is a real man to satisfy me."

Rick's blood was running cold. Stunned by the confession, he did not hear Will's excuses or see his hasty retreat from the apartment. He could only stare into space; his mind racing as he slowly realized that Will was offering him a mug of coffee. The television screen was blank, and Will took the disc out of his DVD player and slid it into a cardboard sleeve as he sat down on his settee.

"We've got to do something to help the lad, Rick." Will broke the silence, offering Rick the disc. "We can't let the Petersons get away with this. The lad doesn't deserve this."

No, Lance did not deserve to be used in this way. Staring at the disc in its protective sleeve, Rick reached out and took it. Maybe they could do something about it now, with the help of this insignificant-looking disc. It was providing them with some solid evidence to show to Blake Brookes, and he was not going to appreciate the derisory comments that Cindy had made about him. Beginning to feel more confident, Rick drank some of his coffee. Maybe now they could help Lance to break free.

Chapter 6

Lance was standing in the kitchen as he waited for the kettle to boil so that he could make two mugs of coffee. Cindy had paid someone to thoroughly clean the apartment a few days ago, the thought of tackling the task herself being repulsive to her. Now, though, there was another large pile of crockery stacked in the sink and two sacks of rubbish waiting quietly in a corner to be disposed of. Coffee stains marked the worktop, Lance choosing to ignore them as he made the coffee. Leaving the teaspoon on the worktop, he picked up the mugs, then hesitated for a moment before reluctantly making his way through to the living room.

Sitting on the settee, Cindy's long legs were stretched out in front of her from beneath her silk dressing gown. With Lance's laptop on the coffee table before her, her manicured fingers were hovering over the keyboard as she stared at the screen. Neither of them was making any effort to pick up any of the clothing and paperwork that was scattered about the room.

Putting one of the mugs down onto the table beside his laptop, Lance moved away from Cindy and sat down on the nearby armchair. Apart from the small side table just inside the hall door and the television and DVD player, there were only a few framed photographs in the room, standing on the shelf that ran along one of the walls. Outside, a watery sun was shining and they could hear the wind whistling by the window.

The pair had only just got up, it being mid-morning on a Friday. Cindy appeared to be oblivious to Lance's presence, her eyes remaining firmly on the screen before her. He was too tired to care about what she was doing, though, as he took no notice of her snooping. She had always pried, leaving him with no hiding place for his most private thoughts except locked away in his mind.

"What's all this," Cindy suddenly asked, stopping him from falling asleep, "in your browser history? Something about a King Arthur?"

"What? Oh, he's someone who's supposed to have lived around here years ago. The people here seem to make a big deal out of it, so I thought I'd best research it so that I don't offend anyone while I'm here. Shouldn't you be getting ready? The taxi will be here soon."

Cindy had to reluctantly agree with him. Appearing satisfied with his explanation, she then decided that it all looked very boring. Who cared if anyone was offended by their lack of interest in someone who used to live here many years ago? That was all in the past. He should be concentrating on the present and future instead of looking up some stupid tale that would not affect them at all. No wonder all of the people in this grotty little town were backward and incapable of achieving anything.

Sharply tapping one of the keys, she announced that she had deleted it so that he could concentrate on what really mattered. Lance said nothing. Right now he did not care whether she had deleted it or not. Eyeing him for a moment or two, Cindy got to her feet and picked up her mug of coffee. He was right. She should be getting ready. Hopefully things would liven up when they got to London.

Cindy disappeared out of the room, leaving him to close down his laptop. Stopping just out in the hallway, she peered through the crack in the doorway. Watching in silence, she saw Lance eventually get up and close down his computer. Disappointed and annoyed, she turned and walked away. She had expected him to seek out the information that she had just deleted, and she had failed to get that reaction from him. He really was spineless; really had no fire in him at all. She only needed to bide her time, though. Once Blake's company was hers, things were going to be very different. Then this whole charade could come to an end.

Lance was unaware that Cindy had been watching him. She had expected one reaction, but instead had watched him move over to the window and stare outside. He had no desire to go to London with Cindy. All too easily he could imagine being dragged from shop to shop while she bought clothes to add to the mountain that she already had but had never worn. What he had wanted to do was make his way back to that gorge this weekend. He had wanted to cross that hillside and step into those trees so that he could immerse himself in a time that refused to be forgotten.

Questions quickly formed in Lance's mind. Why could Rick not come up with a way to free him from this nightmare existence? Why was he being forced to spend the rest of his life with Cindy? He could think of only one way to escape, and that was for him to take his own life. It really would be a life not worth living if he was destined to be with Cindy. Now that he had tasted freedom, he knew that he could not take much more. To survive, he needed to escape from this relationship.

Lance had realized that the only redeeming factor of coming to this country had been that he had escaped from Cindy's presence, but now he yearned for more. However, she had followed him over here and had not given him a moment's peace since she had arrived. Not knowing why she had suddenly decided to show such an

47

interest in him was bothering him. He just wanted her gone, and wanted to know how he could get her out of his life for good.

Hearing Cindy's voice, Lance hesitated; then picked up his wallet and keys from the side table and joined her in the hallway. Grabbing his coat, he picked up the two cases that were on the floor and followed Cindy out of the apartment.

Bustling with life and noisy enough to drown out any conversation, Rick and Will were safely hidden in a quiet corner of the railway station platform. They were watching two familiar people who were caught up in the crowds, Rick noting how Cindy climbed up into the waiting train first. Lance was looking miserable and tired, Cindy not waiting for him as he struggled to climb aboard with their two cases. Incensed by what he was watching, Rick now had no respect for the young woman who paraded around as though she owned everything. He could not respect anyone who treated others so appallingly. She was lucky that Lance was not like his father.

The train eventually pulled away from the station, Rick watching it disappear from sight before looking at Will and then moving out of their hiding place. There was nothing to keep them here now, so the pair walked out of the station building and across to Will's car which was old and battered, with one door and the bonnet a different colour to the rest of the vehicle.

Will was not bothered by the car's appearance, but Rick knew that Lance would have recognized it if he had seen it. Yet, no matter what he thought of this car, he had had no choice but to come here in it.

Rick tried to ignore the torn fabric on the seats as he climbed in. Litter was strewn over the floor, Rick cursing silently as he tried to unravel the seatbelt so that he could fasten it. Will climbed in behind the steering wheel, and soon Rick was relieved when they pulled up outside the apartment block. All he wanted to do was climb out of this car and disappear from sight into the nearby modern, red-brick building.

Will, however, was in no hurry, and Rick was frustrated with his relaxed attitude. There was work that he wanted to get done as quickly as possible. Will was gazing up at the building, looking round at Rick when he sighed with frustration. He did not want to loiter any longer. Will hesitated, then hurried after him when he began to walk towards the apartment.

Nervous, Rick pushed a key into the lock of the door before him. Shiftily looking up and down the corridor, he warily opened the door and stepped into the apartment. Will was right behind him, taking no notice of Rick quickly closing the door as he looked about the gloomy hallway. Nudging him as he passed, Rick moved into the living room. Discarded clothing and paperwork was scattered everywhere, but Rick barely noticed it as his eyes settled upon the laptop that was on the coffee table. Rick could not deny that his heart was thumping loudly and quickly. He was not used to snooping around, and could only wonder how some people could make a living from it as he switched on the laptop. He was going to have to steady his nerves somehow.

A second laptop that was on the settee now caught his eye. Everything about it was different, and Rick suddenly realized that he had made a mistake. The laptop on the table had been manufactured by their company. This second one, though, bore the hallmarks of Jim Peterson.

Rick looked from this second laptop to Will; then turned back to the computer that was on the table. Will appeared to know what he was thinking. As Rick closed down the laptop that was on the table, he picked up the other one and switched it on. He was not disappointed when asked for a password, Will making a couple of guesses before succeeding in accessing the computer. He then sat back, his fingers deftly moving over the keyboard as he began to trawl through the files.

"You've accessed it?" Rick stared at him in disbelief. "You scare me sometimes. How on earth did you manage that so quickly?"

"Allow me some secrets, won't you?" Will replied. "Oh my God! You're not going to believe this, Rick! If you thought what I've just done has scared you, then I have no idea what you're going to make of this."

"Make of what?"

Keen to find out what Will had unearthed, Rick quickly crossed from the window to the settee. Cindy's social networking site had been accessed, and now they could look through the recent conversations that she had had. His heart still pounded and Rick's stomach churned, his blood running cold as the room melted away. Numb with shock and disgust, he was aware of Will pulling a memory stick out of the laptop after he had downloaded all of the conversations.

Rick gingerly checked that the corridor was empty before pulling the door open wider and stepping out of the flat. They had left everything exactly as they had found it, and now they were retreating back out of the building. They were not heading for the office, though, and instead parked up outside Will's terraced house and quickly disappeared inside. Coffee was made, and Rick read through Cindy's typed words as Will made two more copies. This was too valuable to them to lose.

"I can't believe any of this," Rick commented, mug of coffee in his hand. "I mean, just look at what she and this other person are planning to do to Lance."

"Yes, it's definitely worse than you having a key cut for his apartment without him knowing.

How the other half live, eh? Can you believe that complex he's living in?"

"Would you want to be in his shoes?" Rick countered.

Will did not need to answer that question. He had not forgotten his recent meeting with Cindy, and now having read what she planned to do to Lance, in his shoes was the last place he wanted to be. He had been as shocked as Rick at what he had read, and he was now attempting to distance himself from it by trying to convince himself that they were helping Lance to escape from that fate. Coupled with the DVD of Cindy's confession to Will, surely even Blake Brookes could not deny what was really being planned. If this did not save Lance, then nothing would.

Chapter 7

The sun was shining outside, the weather quiet and serene. It was Monday morning, and Rick looked up as Lance walked into the room. Rick watched in silence as he made his way to his small office; then glanced at Will as he got up and followed Lance.

Lance was standing by the window when Rick joined him and closed the door. He was staring at the building across the street, the warm weather doing nothing to lift his spirits.

Lance looked exhausted, and Rick sensed that he had completely withdrawn into himself once more. He took no notice when Rick appeared beside him, instead continuing to stare at the building opposite. He was clearly in no mood for idle chatter. He was in no mood for anything at all. He had come here to work, and that was exactly what he was going to do.

"Lance—" Rick began.

"I'm not staying at home with her," Lance immediately interrupted. "I don't care that she's going back home tomorrow. I've already had two days off since she arrived. I couldn't stand another day with her; especially with the way she's acting at the moment. I'm staying here and getting some work done."

Rick had been caught by surprise by Lance's abruptness. It was clear that he would get nowhere if he tried to argue with him. Choosing his words carefully, he suggested that they sat down and made a start. The defiance in Lance's eyes suddenly vanished, and he looked defeated as he turned away from the window and moved across to his desk. Starting the computer, he hung up his coat and fidgeted on his chair in order to get comfortable; then tapped a few keys.

The office was small yet uncluttered. Blake Brookes was a very practical man. He had never seen any reason to have anything more than was absolutely necessary. On the rare occasions when he actually came here, he had everything that he needed. There were more chairs than he needed, the extra chairs soon annoying him. Three would be more than adequate – not the six that were lined up against one of the walls. A large desk stood near the window, making the most of the sunlight that shone in behind him. He had his computer, his telephone and a rarely-used notepad and pen. He needed nothing else.

From his chair Blake could work unhindered, with everything that he needed within easy reach. He could also see into the main office and ensure that his staff were also working. If not, he could easily summon them into the apparently vast expanse of empty office between the door and the desk. It made them vulnerable; put them at a disadvantage. Though he could see them clearly, they had the sun shining into their eyes and therefore were unable to see the expression on his face. Now Lance was here sitting in Blake's place, and he had all of this at his disposal.

Rick watched Lance as he started to access various files. Today he appeared determined to prove that he could concentrate on work when he wanted and needed to. That determination, however, was preventing him from seeing that Rick was silently watching him, mesmerized. He had not seen Lance work properly before. Today he was discovering what he was capable of achieving. Today, he was easily manipulating the available information in order to get what he wanted.

Lance's enthusiasm gradually waned, Rick continuing to say nothing as he watched him eventually rest his head on his arms and fall asleep. Not about to disturb him, Rick moved across to the window. His mind was full of thought after thought. Only one other person was capable of working a computer as quickly and as naturally as Lance had just done. On that one occasion, Will had successfully retrieved an awful lot of evidence that they could use against Cindy. Will's ability he was used to – it had been the thing that urged Rick to convince him to stay after Blake Brookes had so callously and offhandedly rejected Will's business proposal.

Now what he had seen in Lance for that brief period of time convinced Rick that his skill exceeded even Will's natural talent. If they were to work together, then who knew what they would be capable of achieving?

Rick jumped and quickly looked round as the telephone rang shrilly. Lance had already jerked awake, and now he was picking up the telephone. He looked dazed and half-asleep as he finished the call before turning on Rick. Rick should not have let him fall asleep, and certainly should have woken him instead of letting him sleep on.

"You're not going to take anything in while you're in that state." Rick stood his ground this time. "And before you say anything, I'm not going to send you home before the rest of us. We do need to talk though. Come on. We'll grab a coffee and find somewhere quiet."

Rick had taken Lance's coat from its peg, and was now refusing to let him object as he handed it to him. Getting some fresh air might well help him to stay awake. Lance did not move for a long moment or two; then he reluctantly got up onto his feet. He did not want to talk to Rick in the way that he assumed Rick wanted to talk. The only thing that he wanted to hear from Rick was how he could escape from his upcoming marriage to Cindy.

They took no notice of the two receptionists as they walked across the foyer and let themselves out of the front of the building. Heading along the pavement, they soon let themselves into a nearby café. The coffee was bought, the pair then sitting at a small table in a quiet corner. Lance stared at his mug, absentmindedly stirring his drink. Rick was watching him, Lance tense as he waited for him to speak.

After remaining silent for a minute or two, Rick asked what Lance's trip to London had been like. Lance shrugged his shoulders as he kept his gaze upon his mug. As he had predicted, they had gone from one shop to the next. Cindy had spent hours trying on a vast array of clothes before picking out the ones that she wanted to buy. They had been to see a show too, but most of the time she had been as demanding as she had been here.

"No wonder you're exhausted," Rick remarked, hesitating momentarily before continuing, "Lance, you can't go on like this."

Lance refused to look at him as he shrugged his shoulders again. Cindy was due to fly back home in the morning. He only needed to get through tonight. Nothing else mattered except that she got what she wanted. Lost for words for a few long moments, Rick continued to gaze at him. The time was not yet right for him to tell Lance what he and Will had unearthed. Swallowing, he licked his lips and took a deep breath.

"Maybe you should call the whole thing off; refuse to go ahead with the wedding."

Lance looked at him sharply, unable to believe what he had just heard. "I can't do that. My father would never allow it. I have no choice. I *have* to marry Cindy. What I want is not important. I have to get married for the benefit of the company."

"Oh, hang the company, Lance! Just look at you. It's not worth you suffering like this. It'll be the death of you if you're not careful."

Lance looked away as Rick continued with a calm but firm voice. Lance was not to come into work tomorrow. He would send Graham over with the car in plenty of time to get Cindy to the airport. Once Lance had watched her catch her flight, Graham would take him straight back home so that he could get the sleep that he clearly needed. He was no good to anyone while in this state.

Rick cut in again, stopping Lance when he began to object. This time he was not going to argue with him, and he did not care what Lance's father might say if he was to find out. Lance desperately needed to sleep. Everything would be arranged with Graham as soon as they got back to the office, and once he had finished work tomorrow, Rick was going to call round so that he could find out how Lance was.

Lance felt too tired to argue anymore. He sighed as he pulled his door keys out of his coat pocket and told Rick to take one in case he needed to let himself in. He could not deny it any longer. He was feeling incredibly tired. Rick could obviously sense that, and so he would never believe him if he tried to claim otherwise. He had no idea why Cindy had come here and behaved like a woman possessed. She had always made it perfectly clear that she could barely tolerate his presence.

Lance had not noticed how Rick had hesitated before taking the keys from him. Rick took one of the keys off the key ring, and Lance took the other back and returned it to his coat pocket. It was time that they returned to the office so that they could get some work done.

Lance reluctantly closed down the computer when they had finished work for the day. He was not looking forward to going back home. He wished that he could stay here tonight; that he could wait until Cindy had gone before returning to the apartment. The harsh reality was that he had to go home, though. He had to spend one more night with Cindy before being left in peace. Taking a reluctant step towards the door, he stopped and looked round at Rick upon hearing him utter his name.

"Lance, try standing up to Cindy. I have a feeling that she wants this wedding to go ahead far more than we realize. I have a feeling that, for some… unknown reason, she wants to keep hold of you. And if I'm wrong, what's the worst thing that could happen?"

Lance was totally unconvinced, yet said nothing as he turned and trudged away. Rick watched him go, glancing at Will when Lance had disappeared from sight before returning his gaze to the open doorway. He could not see Lance finding the courage to stand up to Cindy. He feared his father's wrath too much, and having met Blake Brookes, Rick could understand why.

"He's given me a door key so I can let myself in to check him tomorrow," Rick informed his colleague, "and I know one thing, Will. Having seen Lance on that computer today, I believe you'd lose to him in a competition. Cindy has no idea what she's talking about. He's definitely far from inadequate and useless."

Will said nothing. Both he and Rick had seen how domineering and forceful Cindy was. That she should belittle Lance's ability with a computer did not surprise them. Maybe, if he could break free from her, they could demonstrate that ability to his own father. They really needed to show Blake Brookes the evidence they had gathered. As soon as Christmas and the New Year were over, Rick planned to fly over to Boston so that he could confront Blake. After today, he was determined to stop only when Blake accepted that he was wrong to force Lance into this marriage. He was not going to stop until the wedding had been called off.

Chapter 8

Lance hesitated, his hand hovering just in front of the lock of his door. Desperately hoping that he had got the dates wrong and that Cindy had flown home today, he unlocked the door and stepped inside. Cautious and wary, he made his way along the gloomy hallway to the living room door. He was barely breathing as he crept forwards. Please let the apartment be empty. Please let him find himself all alone.

Cindy was sitting on the settee, her own laptop on the coffee table before her. Lance's laptop had been pushed to one side in order to make room, the paperwork that had been lying on the table pushed into a heap and onto the floor when the laptop had been unceremoniously moved out of the way. Intent on what was on the screen before her, Cindy took a few minutes to realize that Lance was standing in the doorway. Spotting him at last, she barely reacted as she stared at him before telling him to make some coffee.

Again Lance hesitated before dropping his key onto the nearby side table and taking off his coat. Throwing it over the back of the armchair, he made his way through to the kitchen and switched on the kettle. Stand up to her, Rick had said. How on earth was he supposed to do that? Lance did not dare stand up to her. The repercussions were too dire to even contemplate. If he dared to upset Cindy in any way, his father would be livid. No matter how much Rick might have urged him to, he simply could not do it.

Returning to the harsh reality that was his life, Lance made a single mug of coffee and carried it through to the living room. He said nothing as he put it down on the coffee table beside Cindy's laptop. Then he sank into the armchair and closed his eyes. All that he wanted to do was go to sleep. All that he wanted was for Cindy to leave him alone and let him get the rest that he needed. She was currently busy on her laptop and barely taking any notice of him. This was what their life had been like, and what their life together was destined to be like. Was this really all that he had to look forward to – living with someone he loathed? How could he possibly think about standing up to someone like Cindy?

Lance was on the verge of falling asleep when he was brutally and rudely awakened by Cindy straddling him. There could be no denying the expression of shocked surprise on his face when he was jerked awake. Cindy, however, was clearly relishing every moment of the torment that she was putting him through. She smirked as she reminded him that this was their final night together for some time. And she knew exactly how she wanted to spend it.

"Not tonight, Cindy," Lance dared to say.

Caught by surprise, Cindy initially looked shocked; then angry. "What? Are you turning me down? A real man would not reject me. A real man would not hesitate in giving me what I want. I can't believe that you've said no."

Rick's suggestion was ringing loudly inside Lance's head. Cindy's goading now made him snap. She had not given him a moment's peace since her arrival here. Now he was too exhausted to be able to give her anything. Obviously he *was* too inadequate for her, and he was beginning to believe that it would be best to call the whole thing off and cancel the wedding. She would then be free to find herself someone who would be able to satisfy her.

Cindy's mouth tightened as she stared directly at him; then she stepped back. How could he dare to refuse to give her what she wanted? He had even just dared to suggest that they called off their wedding. Cindy was seething; her anger clearly audible in her voice as she asked him what his father would say if he knew what he had just suggested. How much trouble would he then be in?

"I don't care what my father might say." Lance suddenly got up out of the armchair. "And I don't care if you agree to call off the wedding. Right now, I don't think I want to marry you."

Rick had been right. Everyone was being unfair to him, expecting him to accept this treatment just for the sake of the company. In his brief time here he had already tasted a different kind of life to the only one that he had ever known. If he did not say something now, he knew that he would be destined to live a thoroughly miserable life. Having dared to speak out, Lance now turned and walked out of the room.

Stunned by his outburst, Cindy seethed with indignation as she watched him go. Livid that he had dared to reject her, she followed him out of the room. Stopping in the doorway, she looked up and down the hallway before finding him in the bedroom. Glaring down at him as he lay on the bed, she could not believe that he was already asleep. No-one could fall asleep this quickly, not unless they were as exhausted as he had just claimed. Indignant, Cindy wanted to tell him exactly what she thought of his impudence.

She reached down, intending to shake Lance until he woke so that she could unleash her wrath upon him. She suddenly stopped herself, however, her features twisting as she scowled. She could not speak her mind, no matter how much she dearly wanted to. Nor could she demand an apology for what he had just said. Unpleasant though it was, she realized that she had to go ahead with this marriage. It was the only way that they could get hold of Blake's company and be rid of their opposition for good.

Cindy continued to glare down at Lance for a while longer. She detested him with every fibre of her body. This last week had been far more unpleasant than she could have imagined. Her skin had crawled every time he had touched her. Now she could do nothing but let him sleep. The only redeeming factor was that she knew that she had already done enough to fool him into believing what she wanted him to believe.

Cindy scowled again; then turned and walked defiantly out of the room. She knew that she would have to do something that she had never done before when Lance woke from his slumber. Unpalatable as it was, she was going to have to swallow her pride and actually apologize to him. She could not afford to let him slip through her fingers, not now that they were so close to achieving their goal. Things were going to be so different once they were married. She would then be able to make him pay for the way that he had just humiliated her. Her mouth still set in a tight line, she was determined that he was going to suffer greatly for what he had dared to do.

Rick knocked on the door a second time and waited for a moment or two before pulling the key Lance had lent him out of his pocket and letting himself into the apartment. What Graham had told him earlier was still fresh in his mind.

The atmosphere had been one of relief when he had brought Lance back from the airport that morning. Glad that he knew that Graham had escorted him up to this apartment, Rick looked along the hall as he closed the door behind him.

Lance was standing just outside his bedroom door, and Rick hesitated as he gazed at him. He still looked very tired, and Rick hated Cindy for what she had done to him. He was going to put a stop to this at the first possible opportunity. Now was not that time, though. Right now, he could only usher Lance into the living room and make him some coffee. Handing over one of the mugs, Rick sat down on the armchair and gazed across at Lance. Both were subdued as Rick put his mug down onto the coffee table.

"She's gone then," he remarked, and Lance nodded. "Good job too. How are you feeling?"

"OK, I guess." Lance shrugged his shoulders. "You were right about Cindy. She did not like it when I suggested that we called off the wedding. I was just so tired though. She actually apologized when I woke up. What is it that she wants? Why is she so keen to marry me when neither of us can stand being in the other's company?"

"Maybe she just wants to get hold of your father's company, like you suggested. I've thought about that a lot, but the only way of knowing for sure was for you to call it off." Rick hesitated. "But just so you know, I didn't like

Cindy from the moment I first saw her. She's too cold and full of her own importance for my liking. She obviously doesn't care who she tramples over as long as she can get what she wants."

Lance glanced across at Rick, the hint of a smile on his face. So what was he supposed to do now? He couldn't talk to his father. Blake would never listen – Rick knew what Lance's father was like. Now Lance would not be at all surprised if Cindy went running to his father with some outlandish claim about his behaviour. He really could not see a way out of the fate that he was destined to have.

Rick drank some of his coffee. He believed that they would find a way of freeing Lance. Cindy was over-confident, and that could easily end up being her downfall. Rick believed that they would get an opportunity before Lance was due to return home. Lance looked steadily at him, long moments passing before he looked away and asked where he could buy a car. He wanted to explore this area while he still had the chance, not spend his time sitting here and thinking things through. He wanted to go out to different places, keep his mind occupied instead of thinking of Cindy all of the time.

Surprised, Rick eventually shrugged his shoulders. Maybe, he suggested, Lance could use the company car instead of buying a car for a few months' use. They could find out if it was possible when they were in the office tomorrow, if Lance thought that he would make it into work. Lance nodded quickly, beginning to relax.

Pausing, Rick got up and patted Lance's shoulder as he offered him his key back. Staring at the key, Lance told him to keep it for now. There was no knowing if he might need it again. Rick hesitated; then nodded, forcing a smile before turning and leaving Lance alone once more.

Lance soon began to wonder what he had done, as he pulled away from the apartment block. Everything was so different here. He was not used to the controls being on the opposite side, and was certainly not used to having to use a clutch and gear lever. Rain was falling heavily too, giving him one more thing to worry about as he concentrated on driving on the left. There were already so many different things for him to think about, and the heavy traffic in Bristol only added to the stress.

Lance was feeling lost as he continued to drive along the road. He had checked his route countless times since learning that he could make use of this car, yet still he was feeling uncertain as he followed the road. At last he spotted a sign directing him to the gorge at Cheddar. He eagerly followed it, and at last he started to recognize some of the scenery.

The towering black cliffs of the gorge appeared to close in and threatened to block his path as Lance drove up through the gorge. He rounded a corner and suddenly emerged once more into the open again, though, the countryside stretching away on all sides. Once again the wind and rain buffeted the car, and Lance drove on before eventually pulling over onto the grass verge at the side of the road.

Protected from the rain by his waterproof coat, he climbed to the top of the nearby hill and looked about him. He had not expected to see the trees marking his intended destination so close by. Anticipation was taking hold, and Lance was keen to hurry across and shelter in those trees. He had read more about King Arthur once Cindy had gone and his laptop had become his own once more. Why should he not be interested in a little local history? Arthur may have been labelled a myth, but did it really matter if he was just that? Lance could see no harm in actually believing in this noble warrior. He needed someone to believe in and give him a reason to keep on living.

The wind and rain were gone as soon as he stepped into the cluster of trees. Lance stopped long enough to pull down the hood of his coat as he looked out at the open hillside; then shuddered and turned back so that he could move further into the trees. Drawn forwards by some invisible force, he eventually came across the lake in a large clearing.

Bathed in that eerie white light, the scene before him felt calm. Gazing across to the mist-shrouded island that was at the centre of the lake, he followed the edge of the water before suddenly stopping once again. He was here; he was actually back at the spot where they had stopped and stared across at that island only two weeks ago. The others had suggested that they row over there, and he still had no idea where they had intended getting a boat from. That was a question to which he would never get an answer. That young woman's sudden appearance had put a stop to that.

Lance sat down on the pale grass that was growing beside the banks of the lake, and continued to stare across at the island. He had so many questions that he wanted to ask, and he could think of no-one better than the people who had lived those lives to give him the answers he was seeking.

Engrossed in his thoughts, Lance was unaware of the young woman hiding in the trees behind him. She had been called over by voices that only she could hear, and she had sensed Lance's presence as soon as she had stepped in amongst the trees. Her heart was beating strongly as she watched him. Not ready to reveal her presence, she remained silent and out of sight. Those who lived on the island were calling over to this young man, their words going unheard by him.

Gwyn could hear everything that had been said. She could not blame Lance for not yet being able to hear them, though. She had been drawn to him during his last visit, unable to stop herself from looking at him. She had not dared to believe that he would return, the last two weeks only confirming her fears that she would never see him again. Her excitement was increasing rapidly now though, and she had to fight the urge to move out into the open when he eventually got up onto his feet again. He had spent hours here, Gwyn watching him as he stared across at the island. She had to be patient and remain hidden until told that it was time for her to approach him. Now, as she watched him disappear from sight, she heard those voices claim that they believed they had found the person they were seeking. Biting her lip, Gwyn not help but smile. They so desperately wanted to find the one, and she could only hope that he was that person. With her excitement making her feel lightheaded, she smiled widely as she reluctantly turned and moved away from the clearing. Lance had to be the one they were seeking. She would never recover from her disappointment if he did not prove himself. She needed him to do that.

Chapter 9

A strong wind was blowing the heavy rain that fell onto the open hillside, yet beneath the trees there was shelter and a gentle quietness that could not be experienced anywhere else. Even in the clearing that was bathed in white light, there was no rain. No tree branches were thrashing about, despite the ferocious wind that was blowing beyond the boundary of the wood. There was only an eerie calmness and tranquillity, and a sense that this place belonged to another time.

Hiding in the trees, Gwyn was watching the solitary figure who was sitting on the grass at the bank of the lake. He had returned for the fourth weekend in a row, and each time he had not seen her as she watched him. Just like the inhabitants of the island that constantly changed shape in the swirling mists of the lake, she had sensed his thirst for knowledge and his desire to uncover the truth.

There was something about this place that kept drawing Lance back. It was not just the sense of peace, nor the way that the rain did not reach this clearing. No-one could explain the absence of any weather here. This place left him feeling happy and contented, feelings that he had never experienced before. Here, there was no hostility or demands being made of him. He could soak up the atmosphere for hours, forgetting everything else.

Today, Gwyn could sense that Lance was struggling to connect with her world. He appeared to be distracted by something that was preventing him from reaching out to the island's inhabitants. Today he was finding it impossible to sense the warmth of their welcome. After coming so close to being able to both listen and speak to these ghosts, his thoughts were preventing him from being able to reach out to them today.

Gwyn held her breath as she heard the voices whispering to her. She had been waiting for this signal to move forwards and reveal her presence. She had been warned to remain hidden on every occasion so far. Today, though, the ghosts had realized that their visitor needed help before he lost interest and never returned. Convinced that he was the one they were seeking, they did not want to lose him now. It was time for Gwyn to make her move.

Feeling both excited and nervous with the anticipation of what might follow, Gwyn took a deep breath in a bid to steady her nerves; then moved out of her hiding place and into the clearing. She had not been noticed. Gwyn crossed over to where Lance was sitting, and stopped beside him. Seeing her at last, he quickly looked up at her for a few long moments before scrambling up onto his feet.

Gwyn was saying nothing, instead giving him time to accustom himself to her presence. He was checking her over, appearing to take note of the pale blue dress she wore beneath her green cloak. He appeared to recognize her, and Gwyn was glad that he remembered her. His eyes focused upon her face, her expression calm as she smiled softly.

"Hi," he said at last, his mouth dry as he tried to think of something to say. "I'm Lance."

"I'm Gwyn," she answered, relieved that he had broken the silence, "and we're glad that you decided to come back. We've been watching you."

Gwyn watched him as he eyed her for a moment; then looked about them. There were only the two of them standing on the bank. Smiling knowingly as he gazed into the trees, Gwyn turned away and sat down on the pale grass. Knowing that he was watching her, she patiently waited for him to join her. The introductions had been made. Now it was time for her to find out what she could do to convince him to join them.

"They've been trying to talk to you," she informed him as Lance eventually sat down beside her. "Arthur and Guinevere have been calling across to you ever since you started coming back here. It's not easy to hear them, though. It takes time. They know that something is bothering you today."

Gwyn stared across the lake to Avalon. She was acutely aware of Lance staring at her, his gaze eventually switching to the island; then down to the grass in front of his feet. Gwyn was saying nothing more, instead waiting for him to give her an answer. She could tell that he was reluctant to tell her anything, but then she could hardly expect unguarded honesty from someone whom she had effectively just met.

Lance spoke suddenly, catching Gwyn by surprise. He had just received some unwelcome news that he did not want to discuss, but that was not why he had come here. He had come to discover the real story of King Arthur. He had read all about him, but he wanted to know how true that information was. He had sensed King Arthur nearby, and that he was trying to talk to him.

"Please don't tell me that it's just my imagination," he added. He had become nervous and embarrassed.

Gwyn, however, was smiling in her quiet and unnerving manner as she assured him that it was not his imagination. Arthur and Guinevere were very real. If he learned how to listen properly, then he really would be able to hear them. Gwyn had already anticipated him asking how. Again she smiled quietly while gazing at the island, before eventually looking back at him. He needed to listen with his heart; to show them that he really did truly believe.

Lance's gaze met that of her own hazel-coloured eyes as she watched him intently. She looked so fresh and young that it seemed to be holding him under some kind of spell, until he suddenly swallowed and looked away again. He appeared unable to doubt her, even for a moment. Gwyn had spoken, and felt both pleased and honoured when asked if she would tell him what had really happened. Quelling her excitement, she stared across at the island as she considered her response. Long moments passed until, as Lance started to look away from her, she broke the silence.

"Arthur and Guinevere have been reunited on Avalon. They are safe there, and able to openly display their complete devotion to one another. They are also trapped over there though, and can't leave. The Lady of the Lake, the person who gave the sword Excalibur to Arthur, guards the lake so that no-one can reach them. It also means that she will not let them escape."

The enchantress Morgan was behind everything, Gwyn went on to explain. She had trapped the wife of Sir Pelleas in the lake's waters. She was doing everything she could to help Arthur, but against Morgan's powers, there was not much that anyone could do. The enchantress wanted Arthur for herself, and she had spun a web of lies in her determination to win him. She had sensed that the other knights were jealous of Lancelot's popularity in court due to his ability in battle, and she had therefore told Sir Pelleas that she would free his wife from the lake if he instigated an allegation of treachery directed at Guinevere and Lancelot. The rumours that Pelleas had started in his desire to rescue his wife had increased and refused to go away, and so in the end Arthur had been left with no option but to take action.

So the history books had got it all wrong?

Gwyn smiled quietly, confirming that the history books were wrong about Guinevere and Lancelot. Despite some doubt about Guinevere's integrity, Arthur himself had known that the rumour had been nothing but a lie. He had been prepared to ignore it, but his court had insisted that he took action. Forced to follow Lancelot when he fled back to France, Arthur had hoped that holding a stand-off outside Lancelot's castle would appease his critics. But they were after blood – Lancelot's blood.

Both Gwyn and Lancelot had been engrossed in Gwyn's explanation, and so neither of them heard someone approaching them until he had spoken and made them both look round. The man who had ushered Gwyn away on their very first meeting was now moving out from the trees and stopping before them. Gwyn's stomach had already knotted. She could guess what was going to be said, and she was dreading the comments that were undoubtedly going to be made.

"I hope you're not falling for all of that nonsense," this newcomer remarked with disdain. "Gwyn lives in some kind of fantasy world. She has such a vivid imagination, and she's under some kind of delusion that some ghosts regularly speak to her. Everything that she claims is made up. If you have any sense, then you'll just ignore her."

Gwyn was feeling humiliated, and this newcomer's arrival was both unwelcome and uncomfortable for her. He was gloating openly, as though revelling in her discomfort. For once, she desperately wished that he would just leave her alone. She had dared to believe that she had started to connect with Lance; that she had found someone who was just as eager to believe in what she believed in. Hot and flustered, she could sense Lance looking up at the man who was standing in front of them.

"It is possible that the history books have got things wrong," Lance pointed out, his voice calm and steady, "and so I see no reason why I should not believe what I have just been told. Why should Gwyn not be telling me the truth?"

The smug expression on Gwyn's tormentor's face had disappeared, and Gwyn herself felt surprised that someone had actually supported her. Lost for words, the newcomer was obviously finding it inconceivable that someone could possibly believe what Gwyn had said.

Gwyn quickly looked round at Lance; her surprise abundantly clear as he continued. He had come here with the sole purpose of finding out what the truth was, and he could see no reason why he should not believe everything that he had just been told.

"Well, if that is what you really want to believe." The newcomer was shaking his head. "I was only trying to protect you from Gwyn's fantasy world. You obviously don't want to be saved, though. You obviously want to be sucked into this madness."

He turned away, and hesitated before looking back at Lance. Just so that he knew, he warned, Gwyn was saving herself for Arthur. Lance had no chance, and would get nowhere with her.

Gwyn was blushing brightly, preferring to stare into space instead of at either of the two men. She and Lance were left alone again, Gwyn too embarrassed to say anything for a few moments.

"I'm so sorry about what my brother has just said," she muttered eventually.

"Your brother?" Lance sounded surprised, and Gwyn quickly confirmed that Gareth was indeed her brother. "I'm sorry. I didn't realize that he was your brother. He doesn't seem to treat you very kindly."

Gareth was not so bad, Gwyn claimed as she shrugged her shoulders. He had simply become over-protective over the last five years since their parents had died. She had only been fourteen, and Gareth had just finished school and had been working in their shop in Glastonbury. Their parents were returning from running a stall at a craft fair in Exeter when they were involved in an accident on the motorway. Gareth had taken over the running of the shop, and had become her legal guardian until she had turned sixteen.

Tucking her knees up against her chest, Gwyn stared out across the lake. She knew that Lance was gazing at her, and she sensed the moment when he looked away towards the ground in front of his feet. She was not bothered about revealing what had happened to her. It had felt like a natural thing to do. Having paused, she now continued.

She had looked upon Gareth as a tyrant at first, only changing her mind when he finally admitted that he feared losing her as well. She had always preferred being here, and so when she turned sixteen, he had found her a little house that was not far from here. It had given her the chance to live the life that she had always wanted. Gareth was not so bad, and was certainly nothing like as bad as he liked to portray. It was simply an act, driven by his fear of losing her.

Suddenly, Gwyn looked round at Lance. What about him? She had told him what had happened in her life. Now it was time for him to do the same. Gwyn fell silent, watching Lance as he swallowed and composed himself. There was not much that he could tell her. He was an only child, and his father owned a computer company. The main office was back at home in Boston, and they had a smaller office here in Bristol. He had been sent over here for a year to see how the branch here was run, and then he was expected to return home and eventually take over from his father. He was engaged, and was due to marry the daughter of the man who owned a rival company when he returned home.

"Oh, I see," Gwyn said, deeply disappointed by his revelation.

"No. No, you don't." Lance sounded bitter, her disappointment unnoticed. "I hate her; can't stand the sight of her, but she wants us to get married as much as our fathers do. She came over here to see me about a month ago, and she called me last night to tell me she's having my baby. I definitely have no choice but to marry her now."

Gwyn said nothing as she gazed at him. The bitterness in his voice had surprised her. Lance glanced across at her before quickly looking back at the mist-shrouded island. Gwyn could see that he was now the one who was feeling embarrassed.

"I'm sorry," Lance apologized, "I don't usually go round telling people about myself. I don't know why I just did. It's got nothing to do with why I've come here. I'd still like to come here and find out more, if you don't mind. I do believe that… that *they* were once real."

A quiet voice drifted on the breeze, and Gwyn noticed how Lance quickly looked across at the island.

"*We are real, Lance,*" the voice had whispered. He could not deny it, having just heard every word that had been spoken. There was no-one who could be seen though; only that mist-shrouded island in the middle of the lake.

Gwyn smiled. To be able to hear that voice whispering on the breeze, he had to truly believe. She was not going to refuse to let him return. Her excitement had increased, despite the revelations that had just been made. They needed him to be here and take on the challenges that would face him. Tingling with anticipation, Gwyn announced that he was more than welcome at any time. Hope had been rekindled.

Chapter 10

Weekends became filled with an all-consuming interest, with Lance returning to the shores of the lake at every possible opportunity. Gwyn had already been waiting for him on some occasions, and joined him moments after his arrival on others. They had talked for hours while sitting on the pale green grass, Lance's hunger for knowledge proving insatiable. He wanted to know more, and Gwyn answered all of his questions in detail as she slowly revealed the true depth of her knowledge. There was nothing, it appeared, that she did not know.

Avalon itself was what Lance had wanted to hear about first. Gwyn had smiled quietly, putting him at ease so that he stopped feeling foolish over his ignorance. The ancient Celts, she had told him, had not believed in life and death as they were understood in these modern times. They had believed that their souls passed over to the Otherworld, where they could rest and recuperate before their return to this world once again. It had been widely understood in those times that the Otherworld was either a forest or an island. Avalon, which when translated meant 'island of apples', was King Arthur's Otherworld. That island was where his soul was now waiting for a safe passage back to this world.

Morgan had used her witchcraft to entice Arthur to Avalon. Only when he had rejected her had she conceded defeat and begrudgingly allowed Guinevere to join him. Even Morgan had had to admit that they really were utterly devoted to each other. One would not return to this world without the other. They were waiting for the right person to come along, a person who had direct connections with this area and who would pass all three of the tests that Morgan had set to prove their worthiness. Only then would Arthur and Guinevere be able to return.

The tests appeared impossible to pass, with Gwyn unwilling to reveal to Lance what they involved, but apparently every attempt that had been made so far had failed. It appeared that Arthur and Guinevere were destined to remain on Avalon for all time. Arthur had been such a mighty warrior when he had walked in this world. He had slain many foes, which had inspired all of his knights to perform great deeds and acts of heroism. Some of those deeds had been exaggerated, but the truth was not far from what had been written in the history books.

There was one crusade that had dominated Arthur's later life, and that was his unrelenting quest to find the Holy Grail. Despite Guinevere's pleas for him to remain with her at Camelot,

Arthur's overwhelming desire to claim the Holy Grail for his own had been too great. He had succeeded in that quest in the end, and had found the Holy Grail when he sailed across to Avalon.

Lance looked across at the mist-shrouded island. For a moment or two, he considered claiming it for himself. The island was so close, and within easy reach. All he needed was a boat to get him across to that shore. Then he realized that it could never happen.

Smiling, Gwyn seemed to know what he had been thinking. He had worked out for himself that anyone who did actually make it over to Avalon would never be able to return, and there was therefore no way of proving to the modern world that the Holy Grail did exist. It was safest over there, well out of the reach of anyone intent upon profiting from its existence. Besides, the Lady of the Lake still haunted these waters, and she would never permit the removal of the chalice.

Sir Pelleas, like so many others, had been deceived. He had done everything that had been demanded of him. He had followed Morgan's instructions religiously. The enchantress, however, had refused to release his wife from her watery prison. She had claimed that, although Arthur had been trapped upon Avalon, with impossible tasks set to prevent him from escaping, he still did not belong to her. He still belonged solely to his beloved queen. In her anger and humiliation, Morgan had refused to give up the guardian of the lake until Arthur's successor had been found.

Now someone had come, Gwyn informed Lance, who would hopefully succeed in breaking the spells that Morgan had cast. He was the one they were all looking to, the one who could defeat Morgan.

Lance quickly looked round at her, and after researching her claims, on his next visit he shook his head. He had checked through his family tree. He had looked at his ancestors, and they were all mistaken. He had no connection with this area. His father's family had originated from Liverpool, and his mother's had come from Ireland. He could not possibly be the person who they were seeking.

The disappointment was clear in Gwyn's eyes. Lance could not alter his past, though, and so could not attempt to release these shadows from the spells that had been cast. It did not matter how much Gwyn insisted that Arthur and Guinevere did not make mistakes. Lance could not pretend that his ancestors were people who had once lived here. They needed to accept who he was and focus all of their efforts on finding the right person.

The weekends drifted on, until the day came when Lance was quiet and subdued. Though he had still battled through the strong wind and heavy rain to get here, his thoughts were distracting him. Up until today he had been able to block out all thoughts of the wretched life he led beyond the boundaries of this wood. The warm welcome here had consumed him, leaving him feeling wanted and respected for who he really was. He was unable to feel that today. He had no choice but to confess that he was to fly back home to Boston for Christmas before next weekend, and so would not be able to come here again for a while. Much as he wanted to stay here now, he was being forced to leave. He was to be thrown into Cindy's company again, and would be expected to play the ever devoted and loving fiancé.

Gwyn silently pondered over what he had said for a few moments before apologizing. She simply could not understand how anyone could do something that would so obviously make them miserable for the rest of their life. He had spoken the truth when he told her that she would not understand the position that he was in. Lance glanced round at her.

"My father has a terrible temper," he told her. "I'd be completely disowned if I dared to go against his wishes. I'd be thrown out with nothing and treated like a leper. Where would I go then?"

"You'll always be welcome here," Gwyn said, "and you could stay with me, just until you've sorted yourself out."

"I can't do that." Lance stared at the dark and still waters of the lake. "It's not that simple. My father will hunt me down and force me to go back and do exactly as he demands. I can't just walk away from him and be able to live happily. My father would never allow it. What I'm expected to do was arranged on the day that I was born. It's all so our two companies can be united. What I want is not important, and right now that's enough to make me want to walk straight into the lake and make my way over to Avalon."

Guinevere's voice broke the eerie silence. To serve his father was not his destiny. Would it really be that awful if he stood up for himself for once? Surely it would be better than living a miserable and wretched existence?

Having glanced across at the island, Lance decided to say nothing. As he stared at the ground, his attention was suddenly drawn back to the mist-shrouded island. He had clearly heard Guinevere's soft and gentle voice as she coaxed him to follow his heart. Those whispered words encircled him, swirling around before being carried away on the light breeze that had suddenly sprung up from nowhere.

Gwyn said nothing. She too had heard every word that had been whispered. Lance, however, was the only one who could decide whether he could act upon that advice or not. That suggestion would be so easy to follow while he was here with Gwyn by his side. He had all of their support here. Back at home in Boston, though, he would be alone. How could he possibly make a stand against his all-powerful father then? And Cindy had his father on her side, although she was forceful enough to not need his support. Lance did not stand a chance, not against such domineering people.

Lance suddenly swallowed and got to his feet. He could not do it. Beginning to walk away, he hesitated and reluctantly stopped and looked back round upon hearing Gwyn call out his name. As she stood by the lake, the white light illuminated her like a halo. She truly belonged here, and was part of everything that Lance could see before him. The lake, the mist-shrouded island, that eerie white light that bathed everything including the trees that encircled it all, Gwyn wearing her pale blue dress and green cloak while the white light shone behind her... He was just a mere spectator who had been privileged to be allowed to look in upon this scene. "You will always be welcome here," she had said. He too could be a part of this magic if he truly wished to be.

Lance gazed at her for a few long moments; then he turned and quickly walked away through the trees. With his head bowed and hands pushed deep into his coat pockets, his eyes were firmly fixed upon the ground before him. All too soon he reached the edge of the wood, the heavy rain making him baulk as he stared out at it while the fierce wind drove it across the hillside with a vengeance.

You will always be welcome here. Those words were echoing constantly in his mind. It would be so easy for him to turn back and accept Gwyn's offer of shelter. He knew that that would not be possible, though. His father would seek him out and accuse her of the most heinous of crimes before forcefully dragging him away. He had made a mistake by coming here in the first place. He should have stayed away and forgotten all about this place.

Lance was stopped from moving out into the inclement weather on the hillside by an overwhelming desire to look back round one last time. Gwyn had followed him, and was now standing beside a nearby tree with the hood of her cloak covering her head. Guinevere's words were sounding clearly in his mind as he stared at her. *Follow your heart.*

"I can't," Lance insisted, "my father will not listen. He'll refuse to believe that I don't want to be with Cindy. The company is all he cares about. It's the only thing that matters to him."

"You don't know that for certain if you don't at least try," Gwyn pointed out, her voice quiet and calm. "If nothing else, you'll have let your father know how miserable it'll make you. You couldn't be accused of not saying something when you had the chance then."

Lance gazed sadly at her before looking away again. He could not do that from here. He had to go back home and face his father in person. He could easily guess that his father would then refuse to let him return here again. Instead he would probably keep Lance where he could control his every movement and refuse to let him go anywhere ever again.

Only, Gwyn quietly insisted, if Lance let him do that. Sometimes actions spoke louder than words. Maybe, once he had stood up to his father, he might then start to respect him. It would demonstrate that he could think for himself instead of just obeying orders. And if she did happen to be wrong, then she had already told him that he could always come back here.

Was he really destined to return here instead of spending the rest of his days with Cindy? He could not attempt to free Arthur from his prison, but could he possibly play another role instead? Sir Lancelot had been the bravest and most chivalrous of the knights. He had been respected and admired as he had proved himself to be fearless time and time again. Was it really the time for Lance to show how brave he too could be? Lance gazed at Gwyn, and she was smiling quietly as though encouraging him to do so.

Gwyn believed that he would return. It had been whispered both on the wind and in the water. She believed that he would find the courage he needed and would be free to come back to them. If he really wanted to, he could decide his own destiny. All that he needed to do was to believe in himself and trust his friends. Everything would then turn out exactly as it should. He was the one, though, who needed to make it happen.

Lance stared into space, thinking carefully about what she had said. When he looked back, Gwyn was gone. Swallowing, he reluctantly turned away and moved out into the wind and rain so that he could battle his way across the hillside before seeking shelter in the car. Staring out through the windscreen, he was looking at nothing. The words that had just been spoken filled his mind. He was being actively encouraged to stand up to his father, and the people of Avalon had assured him that they would be by his side, giving him the support that he would need.

Lance knew that this was something that he was going to have to do. This was his one and only chance of getting the life that he really wanted. However, they really did not know what his father really was like. They had no idea of what it had been like for him to grow up in his father's shadow so that he was now unable to do anything but cower before the dictator before him.

Lance started the engine as he gathered his senses. He was not looking forward to returning home. He had not wanted to come here, and yet now he did not want to leave. He wanted to stay here, well away from his father and Cindy. He wanted to stay here, where for the first time in his life, he felt safe. Gwyn had no idea how lucky she was, living here and being able to do anything that she wanted.

Lance had been mistaken when he had assumed that Gareth was her husband. He had been very condescending and had done nothing but ridicule her, and Lance had believed that he was a tyrant, yet Gwyn had revealed a much softer side to him when she had defended him. Those first impressions appeared to have been wrong. Gwyn really was genuinely happy with the life that she lived. He could have that kind of life too, if he really wanted. All that he had to do was find the strength and courage to stand up to his father, and he would discover whether or not he could do that when he returned home. He would reach the point of no return, when his whole future would be decided. Was he destined to cow down, marry Cindy and face a miserable existence, or would he finally make a stand and walk away from it all? Only time would tell.

Chapter 11

With his chin cupped in his hand and his elbow propped on the desk, Lance stared vacantly at the computer screen. He had not heard a word that had been spoken to him, Rick sighing with frustration as he gave up. Lance's mind was elsewhere, and Rick could not think of anything to say to bring him out of his reverie.

Over the last couple of weeks, Rick had sensed that something had happened. Lance's whole attitude had changed completely. He was much calmer, and maybe even happy. Rick was finding it unnerving, not knowing why his behaviour had changed so drastically. As he stared at Lance, he began to wonder if he could find out what it was that had inspired such a change.

"You're miles away," Rick remarked, making Lance jerk back to reality and look round at him. "You're obviously in a place where you'd much rather be."

Lance looked away from him and got up onto his feet so that he could cross over to the window and stare outside. Grey skies were reflected in the windows of the building opposite, and he could hear the brisk wind that was blowing. Lance was taking no notice of the weather or the view from this window though. Instead he could see trees surrounding a lake that was bathed in an eerie white light, and in that lake was an island that was partially hidden by an ever-shifting mist. A woman was standing by the water's edge, her full-length dress and green cloak familiar to him. With a hint of a wistful smile, Lance refused to look back at Rick.

"You'll only laugh," he accused.

Rick had twisted around in his chair as he watched Lance move across to the window. Licking his lips, he took a deep breath. Maybe, if luck was on his side, he might get a glimpse of what was going through Lance's mind.

"Go on, tell me. I promise that I won't."

Lance momentarily glanced round before beginning to talk. He had said very little when Rick laughed in shocked surprise.

"I knew you would!" Lance stated. "I knew you'd laugh. That's why I didn't want to say anything."

Quickly, Rick got to his feet and crossed over to where Lance was standing. He could only apologize, admitting that it had been wrong of him to laugh before urging him to tell him everything. Refusing to look at him, Lance continued to stare outside. He did not want to say anything more, fearing being ridiculed further if he did.

Rick was cursing silently to himself. How could he have so stupidly laughed when Lance had dared to begin to tell him? Rick could now see how insecure he was. His mind was racing as he continued to encourage him to talk. Eventually Lance gave in, Rick's relief unseen by him as he refused to look at him while he spoke. Remaining silent, Rick listened.

Lance suspected that they had all guessed that he had not wanted to come over here last summer. He had never been here before, but he had already decided before arriving that he was not going to socialize with any of them. He had been determined to hate it here. It would not upset him then when he finished the year here. Now that he was here, though, he did not want to return home to Boston. He could not bear the thought of being back with Cindy again. He wanted nothing more than to remain here.

Everything had changed on the day that they had stumbled across the lake in that wood. The woman that they had encountered there had unnerved him at first. He had then become curious and had researched King Arthur on the internet. What he read had only confused him, though, so he had decided to return to the lake once Cindy had returned home to see if he could make any sense of what he had researched. That was the real reason behind him wanting a car.

He had gone back there every weekend since then, and had eventually met the young woman again. Gwyn was her name; short for Gwyneth. Gareth, her brother, was the man who had been with her. Their parents had died when she was fourteen, so he had been her legal guardian for two years. That was when he had found her a small house that was next to that wood. She spent her time creating new tapestry designs, which her brother sold in the shop in Glastonbury that they had inherited from their parents. Despite that, she had been kind enough to spend the time needed to explain everything that he had wanted to know about King Arthur. She knew so much about him, and she had made so much sense out of the muddle in his mind. She was waiting for King Arthur to return, so that she could be reunited with him again—

"Lance, I'm not sure that—" Rick was more than a little concerned, but Lance took no notice of the expression that was on his face.

"What's wrong with two people talking to each other? My talking to Gwyn is no different to you talking to any of the women in the office. We've hidden nothing from each other. She's waiting for someone to return, and she knows that I'm engaged to Cindy. All we've ever done is sit and talk about King Arthur."

Rick could do nothing but reluctantly agree with Lance on this occasion, though he could not imagine Cindy seeing the innocence of a purely platonic friendship. With Lance having fallen silent, Rick urged him to continue. Having been glaring at Rick during his outburst, Lance was now reluctantly talking again.

Last weekend, Gwyn had told him that she could not understand why he was marrying Cindy when he detested her so much. Gwyn had no idea what his father was like, and she could not understand how he could be forced into doing something like that simply to benefit the company.

Rick watched Lance carefully, knowing that he could sense being watched. Lance hesitated yet again, Rick wishing that he would look at him as he plucked up the courage to speak.

"I have a feeling that I won't be coming back here after Christmas. Gwyn's right about one thing: I'm going to have to say something to my father. I'm going to have to tell my father that I hate Cindy and don't want to marry her. I know what his reaction is going to be. He's going to be livid, and I can't see him letting me go anywhere unless by his side. I can see me being forced to marry Cindy, especially now that I've got her pregnant. I'm well and truly trapped."

Somehow Rick managed to resist the overwhelming temptation to tell Lance everything that he knew. Succeeding in biting his tongue before blurting it out, he was grateful that Lance had not noticed the way that he had almost spoken. Lance had spoken about standing up for himself and actually confronting his own father.

Rick was, however, feeling compelled to say something.

"It might never happen," he suggested.

"Oh get real, Rick! You've met my father; you know what he's like. Just like you know what'll happen if I called him right now and told him: he'd catch the first available flight over here and frogmarch me back home. It'd be best if I waited until I'm back in Boston, so I can tell him face to face. At least this way I'll not be dragging anyone else into it. I don't think I'll cope with being with Cindy for the rest of my life, though. I'll have to get back here somehow, so I can make my way to the one place where I feel safe. I'll go to Avalon. I'll walk into that lake and not come back out."

Rick was panicking as he stared at Lance in shocked disbelief. He was still so young, and was due to turn twenty-one next summer. He could not simply throw his life away like that.

Unable to look at him, Lance sounded calm as he asked what else he could do. Rick knew as well as he did that his father would not listen to him. Despite knowing that, Lance also knew that he was going to have to go back to Boston and find the courage to confront his father. Somehow or other, he would then have to get a flight back here. His father was not going to accept his decision, though. He would not have got where he was now if he'd allowed others to call the shots. There was no denying that he was a formidable force. Lance, however, could not face being forced to go back to his father and comply with his wishes. So what else could he do?

"If what you fear does come true, I want you to call me as soon as you can," Rick told him, scribbling his telephone number onto a slip of paper. "And please don't go straight over to Avalon. I want you to call me first, so I can pick you up from the airport. If you can't return, then I'll fly over to you. One way or the other, I'll talk to your father. If we can get you back here, then I'll not let your father take you back to Boston. That much I can promise you. Sure, I'll be guaranteed to lose my job, but I'm not prepared to work for someone who can treat his own son in this way. We'll set up on our own somewhere and sort out the legalities to let you stay and work here. I just want you to promise me that you won't do anything silly, but will call me first."

Lance swallowed as he glanced across at Rick. He still preferred to stare out of the window, though. It had started to rain, long streaks of water marking the glass before him.

"I can't do that, Rick. I'm sorry, but I can't promise you anything. I don't know what's going to happen, so I don't know what state I'll be in when I return, if I do return. I can't make a promise that I might not be able to keep."

Rick placed a hand on Lance's shoulder and squeezed it. Lance was nothing like his father, as they had all imagined he would be. Rick did not want to see him getting hurt. He had meant what he had said about Cindy – she was too hard and self-obsessed, and Rick was determined to work something out and get Lance's father to see sense. He had to make Blake Brookes realize that the company was not worth sacrificing his son's personal happiness for.

Lance managed to force a weak smile. He had forgotten about the baby that Cindy was expecting. Rick, however, was quick with his answer: Lance had not asked her to come over here and get herself pregnant. He had the impression that her sole intention for coming here had been to trap him in this way. Rick was siding with Gwyn when she claimed that Lance should not let Cindy ruin his life, and now Rick believed that Lance should stand up to his father and then retreat back here if he needed to.

Rick noted the weary smile that Lance was forcing. And to think that Lance had hated them all when he first came here... Despite his behaviour, they had all welcomed him, and realizing that he had been wrong, he did not know that he deserved their friendship or help.

Putting an arm around his shoulders and guiding him back over to the desk, Rick could sense that Lance had begun to relax. He was not interested in work, though. He wanted to hear more about Gwyn, and how she had succeeded to convince him to at least attempt to stand up for himself. Having met Blake Brookes in the past,

Rick was in no way deluded about the tyrant that he was.

Rick had assumed that Lance would be equally hard, cold and tyrannical. He could not have been more wrong. Time had helped him to realize that Lance had grown up in his father's shadow, and obviously feared him far more even than anyone else did. He had been dominated by the tyrant since the day that he had been born. He had been defenceless then, and had been easily moulded into the person that he now was. The truth was that there was no escape for him from an overbearing and domineering father who demanded nothing but absolute and unconditional obedience. At least the rest of them could escape by leaving the company. For Lance, however, that was simply not an option.

Rick remained silent as he watched Lance leave at the end of the day. Tomorrow he would be flying back to Boston. How long it would take him to muster the courage to attempt to break free, Rick did not know. He could sense that something was going to happen over the next few days, though, and he needed to be prepared to fly over earlier than planned, in case Lance failed to escape. There was, however, no certainty that Lance would call Rick. Of one thing Rick was only too aware: there was no telling what Lance was likely to do.

Chapter 12

Lance hesitated for a moment after the car had come to a stop, then he opened the door and climbed out. A cold wind hit him as soon as the door was opened, and it now continued to chill him as though reminding him of how low the temperature usually dropped here. The acres of glass in the large house standing before him looked dark in the weak December sunshine. It all looked so familiar, having not changed at all while he had been away. Why should anything have changed? Though it felt much longer, he had only been away for three months. And now that he was back here, it felt as though he had not been away at all.

Adrian, the chauffeur, had also climbed out of the car, suddenly appearing beside Lance as he handed over his two small bags. Lance looked at them blankly for a moment or two, and then he sighed and thanked the driver for bringing him home. No doubt his father wanted the company car and its driver back at the office without delay. Collecting Lance from the airport was certain to have been an inconvenience.

Stepping away from the car, Lance looked across at the house again as Adrian headed away, back up their long driveway. He was thankful that he had been brought here instead of to the office. His father would have undoubtedly decided that he would be a hindrance while he was preoccupied with work. Lance did not care what his father was thinking. He had his own thoughts distracting him as they span around in his head. Confronting his father was not going to be easy, if it was going to be possible at all.

The layer of snow that covered the large expanse of lawn surrounding the house was glinting in the sunshine. There were no footprints disturbing it, the snow gleaming white and fresh. Trees were surrounding them, giving the impression that they were completely isolated here. The neighbouring houses might just as well be a million miles away.

Lance noted the three cars that were parked by the house, his own standing exactly where he had left it when he had been sent away. Recognizing the other two, Lance knew that his mother and Nina, their cleaner and cook, would be indoors. Unsure that he wanted to join them, he reluctantly walked across the snow-covered drive and let himself into the house. A blast of hot air hit him as soon as the door was opened, Lance quick to close it again once he had stepped into the entrance hall.

"Lance? Is that you?"

Putting his bags down, Lance looked across at one of the doorways as his mother appeared.

"You're here then," she remarked. "Your father's already booked your flight back. The ticket is up in your room. I'm afraid he's not given you much time to spend with Cindy, though I suppose the business has to come first. She's coming over tomorrow to see you, while your father and I are visiting his brother. You'll have the whole day to yourselves. She's got quite a bump already. You'll see that for yourself tomorrow."

Lance said nothing, instead taking off his coat and hanging it up while his mother continued to talk. He did not want to see Cindy; nor did he want to be reminded of how she had trapped him. He wanted this Christmas to be over, so that he could return to England and never have to come back here. He wanted nothing more to do with Cindy or his parents.

Mrs Brookes called Nina, asking her to bring them two mugs of coffee as she turned back into the living room. Still Lance said nothing as he hesitated before crossing the large and sparsely-furnished entrance hall to the living room. Stepping through the doorway, he stopped and looked about the room. Nothing in here had changed in his absence. It all looked exactly the same, the room reflecting his father's brashness.

Large and luxurious leather sofas and armchairs stood around the imposing fireplace.

Logs were burning in the hearth, while another pile of logs was stacked beside it ready to be added when needed. Framed photographs of his father stood along the solid wooden mantelpiece, above which a large pair of antlers took pride of place. Commissioned paintings hung on the walls, interrupted only by an enormous plasma television on the wall that was opposite the door; its sound drowning out the noise of the burning logs as they crackled and threw shadows over the large, smoked glass coffee table that stood inside the semicircle of sofas and armchairs.

Mrs Brookes was already putting the last of many brightly-coloured parcels under the large pine tree that stood by one of the two windows. She had been shopping in Boston when Lance's plane had landed, and had only just got back herself when Adrian had arrived with Lance. The many lights that were on the tree were sparkling constantly and reflecting off the abundance of tinsel and colourful baubles. The tree was real, the scent of pine intermingling with the smell of burning logs.

Lance at last moved further away from the door as Nina entered the room and put two mugs of coffee down onto the smoked glass table. Christmas cards were everywhere; spilling out from every available space and reflecting the vast number that Lance's mother sent each year. She liked to be popular, and her desperation to be liked was a little too obvious. To Lance, though, the whole house looked so brash, overbearing and all-powerful, as though daring anyone to challenge them. It all signified a great wealth, a wealth that his father had amassed thanks to the sweat and toil of the minions that he oversaw. After his brief time in another country, Lance detested all of this even more.

A telephone call gave Lance the chance to escape his mother's company. Silently slipping out of the room as she took the call, he picked up his bags, climbed the wide and sweeping staircase and disappeared into his room. Immediately homing in on the aeroplane tickets that were on his dresser, he picked them up. He wanted to hear no more talk of Cindy and the baby.

Lance focused upon the date on the tickets. The second of January. He was being forced to wait until then before being allowed to return to England. Almost two whole weeks before he flew back to Bristol… it might as well be a lifetime away. How was he going to survive until then? Lance suddenly smiled knowingly; a warmth spreading through him as he put the tickets back down. He heard Guinevere's voice clearly as she assured him that they were still with him.

Crossing to his window, Lance stared out at the trees that surrounded the house. Arthur and Guinevere were still with him, as though they were standing right here beside him. They were remaining true to their word, and appeared to be the only ones who could hear him screaming out for the help he needed to escape this existence. Why did he have to be the one who was trapped here? He appeared to have everything; appeared to be the luckiest man on earth. The reality could not be more different. If only he could make his voice heard; if only he could be brave, just like one of the noble and legendary knights.

Lance's mother interrupted his thoughts when she joined him. More than a little reluctantly, Lance returned to the living room with her. He stood silently at the far end of the fireplace, looking round only when the headlights from a car shone through the windows and into the room. His father had arrived home, and Lance shuddered as he gazed across at the living room door. All too soon a tall and powerfully built man let himself into the house and entered the living room. He was wearing a three-piece suit, his steel-grey hair mimicking his hardness of character. There was no denying that he demanded humility and reverence from anyone he deemed worthy enough to grace him with their presence.

"You're home then," he stated emphatically, carelessly throwing his coat across one of the armchairs as he moved across to the fire. "I trust your mother has told you that Cindy is coming here tomorrow. I see no point in telling you to behave appropriately after what you've done."

Humiliated, Lance looked down at the floor. He always felt ashamed and inadequate when in his father's company. How could he possibly stand up to this giant of a man? His mind instantly filled with countless memories from his childhood; the recollection of how he had had to quickly learn servility still painful.

"There's no point in you returning to England after Easter," Mr Brookes continued, and Lance looked back up at him. "You'll be getting married then. You'll stay here and work with me, so you'd better make sure that you've made the expected progress by then. I shall be extremely disappointed in you if not."

Guinevere's words rang clearly inside Lance's head. Again she assured him that they were by his side with their support as she urged him to follow his heart. All of the courage that he had mustered had quickly drained out of him as soon as his father had stepped into the house, though. He was not like King Arthur. He was weak and worthless, not deserving to be in such noble company.

Mr Brookes' voice filtered back into Lance's mind again. No-one dared to interrupt his father. Thankfully, he was expected to listen. Still that voice was screaming inside his head. He did not want to marry Cindy. He wanted to go back to England and remain in the court of King Arthur in Camelot. He wanted to spend his days talking to Gwyn.

The one-sided conversation continued after they moved into the dining room. Lance tried desperately to concentrate as he was told exactly what was expected of him. He did not want to invoke his father's wrath, but Guinevere's words were still echoing inside his head as if to directly challenge his father. He could concentrate on nothing, the distraction forcing him to grow increasingly nervous and agitated.

"Blake, Lance is obviously tired after his flight," Lance's mother interrupted, "and it's starting to get late. You can discuss business some other time. Go on, Lance. Go up to your room."

Lance looked warily at his father, moving only when given his permission. Rarely did his mother dare to interrupt his father. Except for Cindy, she was the only person who ever did so. Feeling his father's eyes burning into his back, Lance left the room.

"You're far too soft, Nancy," Blake scolded. "He needs toughening up if he's to succeed in business. At least Cindy has the drive and energy that's required. I'll be leaving my business in safe hands with her once the two companies have merged. We will be invincible then. I know that Cindy possesses the ambition needed to succeed."

"What about Lance?"

"Don't bother me with Lance. He's proved to me time and again that he's totally incapable of doing anything. He's an embarrassment. In fact the only thing he's useful for is his marriage to Cindy Peterson. I'll get her father's company then. He's not good for anything else."

Lance climbed the stairs and shut himself in his room. Leaning back against the closed door, he closed his eyes in a bid to steady his nerves; then crossed over to his window so he could stare outside. He had been meant to hear every word that his father had just uttered. Blake could not help but use every possible opportunity to ensure that Lance knew how inadequate he believed he was. Not a single day had gone by without him hearing at least one derogatory comment.

A full moon was shining outside, lighting up the snow that covered the lawn and trees. Lance could easily imagine Guinevere among those trees. Eleven more days before he was due to fly back to England, eleven more days before he would be able to see Gwyn again. It was too long, was far too long. He could picture her now. He could see her gentle eyes and her soft skin. What he would do to be able to reach out and actually touch her. He had been able to resist that temptation so far. She was, after all, betrothed to the mighty King Arthur, and he was engaged to Cindy. A sense of frustration and helplessness was rising up inside him, and Lance knew that he was going to have to somehow find the courage to stand up to his father.

Lance suddenly looked round as he heard his father's booming voice on the landing. Swallowing with fear and dread, he dared not move. The voice eventually faded, and Lance closed his eyes as he heaved a sigh of relief. He had to get away from this constant torment. He had to follow his heart and somehow get back to Avalon. He had to muster his courage and confront his father. The alternative was something that he did not want to contemplate. Tomorrow, he had to fight to escape. If not, then it would only prove what a worthless coward he was. Gwyn had been right. He had to say and do something, even if it meant that he died in the attempt. At least then he would be free.

Chapter 13

The house was silent; Lance the only one who was at home. He was standing at the end of the fireplace, knowing that it would only be a matter of time before his parents returned. The lights on the tree were glistening off the baubles and tinsel, Lance seeing nothing as he stared into space. He had dared to take that step; to cross that line, and now there was no return. He had to follow through from what he had said to Cindy. There were no other choices now.

At last a car came rushing up the driveway, Lance's stomach tightening as he looked round. He had not expected his parents to return so soon, and suddenly realized that Cindy must have called his father. Nerves were beginning to take hold, and Lance felt certain that he wouldn't stand a chance. He was beginning to tremble, the deep breaths that he was taking doing nothing to steady his nerves.

"What the hell do you think you're doing?" Blake demanded. He had burst into the house and immediately spotted Lance standing in the living room. Lurching forwards through the open doorway, his eyes were spitting fire as he stood over his son. "Cindy has called me. How dare you refuse to do as you're told? How dare you disobey me? How dare you think that you would rather be with someone else? I can't believe that you can bring so much shame to my good name."

"I can explain, sir," Lance dared to speak quietly.

Blake responded instantly, lashing out with the back of his right hand; striking Lance across his cheek. The force was sufficient to throw him against the mantelpiece, and dazed and shocked, Lance heard nothing as he slowly steadied himself. He could taste blood from the cut to the corner of his mouth that had been caused by his father's ring. The room was spinning.

"Don't you dare interrupt." Blake's words were filtering through the haze. "I will not tolerate such insubordination, and I will not tolerate what you're intending to do. You are to go straight over and see Cindy right now. You're to do everything necessary to win her back. You are going to marry her. My company's future depends upon it."

Lance felt an overwhelming confidence sweep over him, as though King Arthur himself had possessed him. Suddenly his father was no longer a tyrant, but instead was the one who was truly weak. Courage built up quickly, taking hold until he felt invincible. Gazing steadily at his father, Lance dared to stand up to him.

"That's all you ever care about," he accused. "Your company is the only thing that you have ever cared about. I hate the company. I hate Cindy and I hate my life. But most of all, I hate you."

A raging anger gripped Blake; Lance quickly ducking out of the way and fleeing the room as his father lashed out again. He had not been aware of his mother's presence, and was now only vaguely aware of her speaking up as he raced up the stairs. Shutting himself into his room, he leaned back against his door and closed his eyes. What had he done? How could he have dared to speak out in the way that he had? His father would be livid. Breathing heavily, Lance tried to think of what was going to happen next. What could he possibly do to escape now?

Gwyn was sitting in her simple kitchen, her fingers expertly working on a piece of embroidery. Several thoughts were running through her head, Gwyn smiling quietly as she worked. She had stopped listening to the rain as it beat against her window, and the cold wind that was blowing outside, firmly shut out of the house. Suddenly stopping and looking round, Gwyn put her embroidery down onto the table and got to her feet. Guinevere was calling to her, urging her to cross over to the lake as quickly as possible. She was needed.

Wrapping her cloak around her, Gwyn pulled her hood over her head and hurried across to the nearby wood. Immediately the trees sheltered her as she walked deeper into the wood. Soon an eerie white light was shining out to her, Gwyn hurrying forwards before stopping at the edge of a clearing.

A familiar and lonely figure was sitting close to the banks of the lake. He was staring into the black and frigid water, his hands pushed deep into his coat pockets as he shivered with cold. The wind and rain out on the hills had soaked him. Gwyn stepped out from her hiding place, and a movement in the nearby trees caught her eye, making her immediately look round at an unknown man, who stared back at her. Gwyn held her breath, frozen to the spot as this stranger urged her to continue. He was prepared to keep back out of sight, letting Gwyn approach Lance.

A silvery and familiar voice travelled on the breeze, Gwyn looking across at the island as she listened. Guinevere was calling to her. This stranger was a friend and ally who could be trusted. He knew that Lance would tell her everything, and he wanted to hear what Lance had to say before revealing his presence.

Gwyn looked back at the stranger hidden among the trees. She could trust Guinevere, and so focusing her attention on Lance, she silently crossed over and sat down beside him. Their eyes met for a few long moments before he turned his face away. It was too late. Gwyn had clearly seen the cuts and grazes that covered his face. He was clearly cold and soaked to the skin, shivering as he stared into the cold, dark water. Despite the tension, there was also a sense of comfort at being once more in each other's company.

"I'm sorry. You said that your father would not like you to speak up."

"You're not to blame," Lance spoke quietly. "You couldn't possibly know what he's like. You were right. I had to say something."

He sounded tired, and appeared reluctant to tell her what had happened; yet somehow he was telling her everything.

"I called the airline and was able to change the booking. My parents were arguing, so they did not see me leaving. I managed to make the flight by the skin of my teeth." Lance swallowed, his eyes fixed on the water as he paused for a moment or two. "It's only a matter of time before they find out that I've gone."

"They already know," Rick spoke up at last, emerging from his hiding place. "Your mother called me. The police found your car at the airport, and the airline confirmed that you'd caught the flight. Your mother called me just before she and your father boarded their flight in New York, so they'll be on their way over here by now."

Lance stared at Rick. He had got up onto his feet when Rick had joined them, and slowly the words that had been spoken were registering in his mind. Taking a step back, Lance shook his head. He was not going to let his father come over here and take him back to Boston. He could not face the life that his father had planned for him. That left him with only one option. He would have to go to the one place where his father would not be able to follow. He would have to make his way across to Avalon.

Lance turned and had taken a couple of steps towards the lake before Rick snatched hold of his arm. Initially struggling, Lance looked back round at Rick when he realized that the grip upon him was not going to be released. Gwyn had moved back, as though not wanting to get involved in this skirmish. She had fallen silent, letting Rick attempt to convince Lance not to enter the frigid water.

"Lance, I promised that I would not let your father take you back." Rick sounded a little panic-stricken. "I'll talk to him, and give him no choice but to listen. If he still refuses to listen, then I promise that I'll bring you straight back here. Can you at least give me the chance to do that?"

Lance shook his head. They both knew that Blake Brookes listened to no-one. There could be no talking to him. He was the one who did all of the talking, while everyone else was expected to obey his orders. Lance knew that his father's mind would already be made up, and that anything anyone might say was not going to change it.

They would never know, Rick pointed out, if they did not at least try. Lance had no ready answer, suddenly feeling a little uncomfortable as Rick eyed him before asking why he had not called him. Lance looked down at the ground. He was no longer attempting to struggle free, and he gave no reaction when Rick's grip relaxed a little.

"I forgot to bring my cell phone. I realized that I'd left it behind when I got off the plane here. I'd forgotten your number and my key for the apartment, too, and I don't know where you live so I got a cab from the airport to the gorge and walked from there."

Rick gazed at him, and then he put his arm around Lance's shoulders. He had a key to Lance's apartment, he reminded him, and could take him home and stay with him so that he could talk to his father when he arrived.

Lance immediately pulled away from the arm that was encircling his shoulders. No matter what Rick might promise him, he was not ready to trust in anyone right now. He wanted to stay here, safely hidden away from his father.

Rick gazed sadly at Lance, shaking his head. He needed to be sure that Lance was safe, and he could only do that by remaining with him. Lance looked across the waters of the lake, and hesitating, Rick followed his gaze. Someone was walking towards them across the surface of the water, and Rick caught his breath; rendered speechless. The woman looked just like Gwyn, and yet she was standing close by on the grass. Not understanding what was going on, Rick eventually noticed how calm and accepting Lance was as he gazed at the approaching figure.

Guinevere stepped off the waters of the lake upon reaching the grass bank, and her bare feet were once again covered by the skirt of her pure white dress. A silvery fabric belt encircled her slender waist, its long ends hanging down in front of her before disappearing into the folds of her skirt. A simple silver band kept her long, light brown hair away from her face, and her skin was pale, her eyes twinkling kindly as she smiled. When she stopped before Lance, both he and Rick could see her gentle and regal quality as she gazed directly at Lance.

"It is not the time for you to make your journey over to Avalon," she said, "but you will be perfectly safe. Your father will listen. You only need to trust the people who are here with you. To defeat your demons, you first need to face them. Stand up to your father one more time, and your remarkable courage will be shown again."

Lance gazed steadily back at her. He could not believe that his father would listen. He could only envisage his unceremonious departure from this land, never to return. Guinevere's presence was calming him, though, and he swallowed as he reluctantly relented. Still uncertain and insecure, he let Rick guide him away from the only sanctuary that he knew. Leaving the shores of the lake, he could sense Arthur and Guinevere walking alongside them. Forced to stop running away, he had to face his father once more. The tyrant was already on his way, and in a matter of hours they would meet again.

Chapter 14

The hills were covered with thick fog; the chilly wind blowing tirelessly, intermingled with a heavy rain. Rick and Lance baulked momentarily when they stepped out of the shelter of the trees. Lance felt a great temptation to return to the safety of the lake, and Rick looked about them as he struggled to remember where he had left his car. The freezing fog and heavy rain were cutting right through them, the visibility almost non-existent.

Rick had parked his car as close as possible, a numbing panic driving him up the hillside to the trees. Gwyn had stepped into the clearing just as he had arrived, and Rick realized in a fraction of a second that Lance would most likely remain calm if confronted by her alone. He had not been wrong. Remaining out of sight, he had listened carefully to every word that had been spoken. There had been no bitterness in Lance's voice, leaving Rick with no doubts over what he had heard.

Away from the security of the wood, Lance became wary as he and Rick made their way down the hill. The grass was wet and slippery, and Rick was relieved when they reached his car. Lance was saying nothing, and his silence was a little unnerving. Now the trees were hidden in the fog-shrouded hillside, Lance gazing back up at them as Rick unlocked the car. He wanted to stay here, not travel to the apartment. He had no guarantee that he would return here again.

Guinevere's voice broke through the rising tension inside him. She and Arthur remained by Lance's side, keeping him safe. They were going to protect him. They needed him to remain here. All hope would be lost if he were taken away from them. Lance had no idea how important he was to them. He was valued, and they were going to protect him against every threat.

Lance appeared to be in a daze as he climbed into Rick's car. Rick was feeling nervous, the meeting on the shores of the lake having unsettled him. Relieved to be back in his car, he believed that they would be leaving all of these inexplicable events behind. The heater was soon blasting hot air out at them, the windscreen eventually clearing of the layer of mist as he drove.

The fog slowly cleared as they left the hills behind. The dreary rain continued to fall, though, the strong wind failing to move it away. Rick drove on, crossing the wide and exposed valley that stretched from the foot of the hills before reaching the outskirts of Bristol. They were back in familiar and normal surroundings, and Rick hoped to banish the image of Guinevere's appearance from his mind so that he could pretend that it had never happened.

Too late, Rick became caught up in the heavy traffic that filled the city centre. There was no escape from the crowds that were swarming tirelessly along the rain-soaked pavements and spilling out of the shops as the final spend before Christmas was well under way. Rick had been about to join this throng when he answered the call from Lance's mother. He had at least been spared this torture, another taking its place.

Rick had gone cold when Nancy Brookes had called him. He had struggled to quash the rising panic, her words slowly sinking in as logical reason gripped him. He had known where to find Lance, and had driven straight to the lake in the wood. Having feared that he would already be too late, he had then seen Lance sitting on the grass and felt annoyed and offended that he had not been called. Lance's explanation had been simple, though, and Rick now believed that he would have been called if it had been possible.

Rick was still acutely aware of Lance's silence. Conversation seemed unlikely, Lance instead staring, unseeing, out of the window. He did not want to talk, and Rick had no idea what might be going through his head. He could not help him if he did not know what he was thinking. Forced to concentrate as he drove through Bristol, he reminded himself to be thankful that Lance was not attempting to make a break for freedom.

Distracted by Guinevere's constant reassurance, Lance suddenly looked round. They had parked in the driveway of a semi-detached house, Rick repeating his invitation for Lance to come inside. Lance shook his head. This was Rick's home, and he was not going to intrude.

Reluctantly, Rick warned Lance not to move as he climbed out of the car. There were a few things that he needed to fetch, and he wanted to be as quick as possible so as to give Lance very little chance to flee.

Lance watched Rick disappear from sight; then looked down at his hands. He was holding his passport and wallet, the only two things besides his aeroplane tickets that he had believed that he needed. He had been focusing upon escaping from the house and returning here while his parents had been arguing furiously. What he was going to do once he had arrived was something that he had given no thought to. He had been spurred on by Guinevere's encouraging words, his sanctuary being the obvious place to retreat to. Now he was sitting in Rick's car, with no idea of when or where he would come face to face with his father again.

Rising panic began to shut out Guinevere's words. He could not face his father again. This was complete madness. He should not have let

Rick and Guinevere convince him to leave Avalon. He needed to get back there, where he knew for certain that he would be safe. He could not stay here and let Rick take him to the one person whom he had always feared.

The door beside him was suddenly pulled open, Lance's stomach tightening and churning as he quickly looked round. His father had found him, and was about to make sure that he never disobeyed him again. His life was going to become far worse than it had ever been before now. It was too late for him to escape now. He was trapped; betrayed by those who had wanted him to trust them.

"Let me look at you. My God, what has he done to you?"

Lance's fear and panic subsided. Melissa had opened the door and crouched down beside him, her fingers touching him. Lance quickly looked away.

"I'm sorry. Rick should be with you, not chasing around after me."

"Do you really think that we'd abandon you, especially at this time of year? I only need to look at you to see that you need help. Have you eaten lately? When was your last meal?"

"Yesterday morning, I guess." Lance shrugged his shoulders. Still he refused the invitation into the house when it was offered a second time. He was not going to intrude, no matter how much they might claim that he was welcome. Melissa was proving to be more persistent, stopping only when the back door of the car was opened, startling Lance. He quickly looked round, relaxing a little upon seeing Rick placing a carrier bag onto the back seat. Rick was joining him again, and Lance felt relieved that he could now escape from Rick's wife.

Evasion was quickly denied, however, and Melissa announced that she would prepare a meal for him. Lance was not going to escape that easily, Rick speaking up when he began to object. Melissa was already hurrying back indoors, Lance watching her through the windscreen as Rick spoke to him.

"We won't let your father take you away," he insisted, "and I meant what I said about starting up our own company if the worst happens. Melissa supports us too. We're not going to abandon you."

Lance could not look at Rick. He did not deserve their support, of that he was certain. He did not want to bring them down with him. He was not worth them losing everything. They appeared to be doggedly determined to do just that, though, making it impossible for Lance to argue with them.

Melissa was already returning. She climbed into the back of the car, gently patting Lance's shoulder. Feeling him jump beneath her hand, she bit her tongue and decided to say nothing as he glanced round at her. There was a flicker of panic in his eyes, betraying all of his old fears that were destined to remain unspoken. He appeared to be uncomfortable in their company, as though wanting to be left alone. They could not grant him that wish just yet, though. Only when his approaching confrontation was over could they start to consider fulfilling that desire.

Rick unlocked the door to the apartment; then took a step back and waited for Lance to step inside. He was wary and nervous, Rick somehow remaining patient as he let Lance take his time. He did not want Lance fleeing now. He needed to keep him here until they had at least confronted Lance's father. Lance moved forwards, acutely aware of Rick taking the carrier bag from Melissa as he hovered on the threshold. Melissa was leaving them, and Rick watched her go before following Lance into the apartment.

Everything was still and silent, the apartment warm and dark. The hallway remained dim and gloomy, despite the light having been switched on. Lance had moved further into the apartment, his wariness diminishing a little as he realized that they were alone. His parents had not yet arrived, giving them time before that inevitable confrontation. The living room was in darkness, Lance edging closer to the doorway when he heard the front door close behind him. With his heart leaping up into his throat, Lance quickly looked round. Rick was standing beside the closed door, Lance staring at him as his breathing levelled out again. Rick was still with him, ensuring that he could go nowhere else.

"Do you have any spare clothes here?" Rick broke the tense silence. "Why don't you have a shower, get yourself dry?"

Lance said nothing. Rick was watching him constantly as Lance left his passport and wallet on the coffee table and made his way to the bathroom. Rick remained in the living room doorway. What was going through Lance's mind? He had no idea of the thoughts that might be spinning around in his head. He could at least imagine how much Lance was dreading the imminent meeting with his father. It would take nothing at all to spur him into fleeing again.

Rick had not expected to see the cut to the corner of Lance's mouth and the graze on his opposite temple. The thought that Blake had struck his own son shocked him. Somehow Lance had found the courage to speak out, and now he looked pale and tired, maybe even defeated. Blake Brookes had stooped to a new low, and was still apparently blind to his behaviour. Maybe Rick should not have brought Lance here. Where else could he have taken him, though? There was nowhere else, except for the lake in the wood, and he couldn't leave him there, not in his present state.

Lance became nervous again when Melissa returned. He had expected to see his parents walk into the room with her, and the anticipation of his father bursting in and assaulting him again was very real, making Lance unpredictable. Even though he had Arthur and Guinevere by his side, he could not always hear their reassurances through the haze of panic.

Melissa had been grocery shopping, and Rick helped her to carry the bags into the kitchen as Lance slowly calmed his nerves by taking several deep breaths. Rain was lashing the window behind him, but Lance was unaware of it as he watched Melissa walk into the living room. Nervous and wary, Lance cautiously sat back down on the settee again, staring at the plate of hot food that Melissa had put down on the table. Now she was refusing to move, wanting to see him eat before she would be satisfied to return to the kitchen.

Rick remained with Lance in the living room, keeping his distance as he watched Lance reluctantly eat. His parents' aeroplane was due to land soon. It would not take them long to make their way over here. Lance was growing increasingly agitated, and Rick knew that it would soon become impossible to convince him to stay here. The words spoken by that ghostly apparition were resounding clearly: Lance needed to face his demons if he was to defeat them.

The rising fear appeared to be making Lance deaf to any words of wisdom. Rick's fears were growing with Lance's nerves. There was no telling what he might try to do once blind panic took hold. Rick knew that he had to keep Lance here and make sure that he did not flee blindly into the gathering dusk, but Lance was finding it increasingly difficult to listen, and Rick's desperation was growing.

Rick relaxed only after Lance had swallowed the tablets that were offered to him. Melissa had eventually brought them mugs of coffee, and Rick was at last able to hand the tablets to Lance. For a moment or two it looked as though he was going to refuse them. He had taken them, however, so now Rick could begin to relax.

Outside, streetlights were illuminating the car park. The rain was still falling heavily, though it was not deterring the hordes of revellers who were hurrying past. Melissa was staring out of the window, her mind running wild as she imagined her two daughters soaking up the over-lenient atmosphere that they enjoyed while with their grandmother. She did not want to think what state the house would be in by the time they returned. Wanting to return home in order to restore discipline, she also wanted to stay here and discover the outcome of the upcoming meeting.

The apartment was quiet, the solitary lamp that stood against one of the living room walls dimly lighting the room. Rick was sitting on the armchair, watching Lance silently. Lance's parents would have cleared customs, and would most probably be heading towards them already. Lance was drowsy, and it was now safe for Rick to pull him up onto his feet and guide him to his bedroom. Rick needed to get him out of the living room in order to give him a chance to talk privately with Lance's father.

Melissa looked round and watched when Rick made his move. She said nothing, her curiosity driving her to follow the pair out of the room. She stopped upon reaching the bedroom doorway, remaining silent as she listened to the short conversation between the two men. Lance willingly lay down, his plea to Rick not to let his father take him away clearly heard as Rick covered him with the duvet. He could not bear the thought of returning to Boston and being forced to marry Cindy. He wanted to stay here, in the company of the people who had shown him that they cared.

Rick continued to watch Lance for a few minutes after he had fallen silent. Satisfied that he was at last sleeping, he turned for the door. Rick had not noticed his wife following them, and Melissa noted his surprised expression when he saw her.

"I hope you know what you're doing," she remarked.

"Yes, I do," Rick confirmed. "I know exactly what I'm doing. Just trust me." He wished that he felt as confident as he sounded. He needed to be confident in order to give Blake Brookes no choice but to listen to him. Knowing that Melissa was unconvinced by his remark was doing nothing to help that confidence. They could do nothing now but return to the living room and wait.

Chapter 15

Lance slowly roused from his sleep and eventually opened his eyes. Hazy memories of having woken earlier filtered into his mind. The sun had been starting to rise then, peering out from the horizon and bringing some light into the gloom of the bedroom. He was still in the apartment in Bristol, and the sun was now shining more brightly through the window, although he could hear the sound of rain lashing against the windowpane.

With everything appearing quiet and tranquil, Lance dared to sit up and rub his head. Logic was telling him that his parents must have arrived hours ago. How could he have fallen asleep knowing that they were due to arrive? Night had been drawing in then, but now the sun was providing light through the rain. His parents had to be here, and yet he could not hear his father's loud and domineering voice.

Lance threw back the duvet and got up out of the bed. There was only one way for him to discover what had happened. He was going to have to venture out of this room and search the apartment. With his heart pounding quickly and loudly, the adrenalin that was coursing through him provided him with the energy that he would need if he wanted to flee.

Lance stopped abruptly, his stomach churning uncomfortably as someone appeared in his doorway. His mother was here, standing before him and blocking any possible escape route. His parents had arrived, and he could only assume that they were all still here only because they had not yet been able to get a flight back home.

"Ah, you're awake at last," Mrs Brookes stated. "Those sleeping tablets that Rick gave you really did knock you out. Go and get yourself a shower while I get you some breakfast."

Lance was left alone in his room once more. He felt numb, and found it almost impossible to take in what he had just been told. Rick would not have given him some sleeping pills, would he? Wait – he had handed him two white tablets, and like a fool Lance had taken them without question. It explained why he had fallen asleep at such a nerve-racking time. Rick had deceived him.

Lance looked about him. If his mother was here, then his father had to be here too. There would be no possibility of him being able to slip past them a second time. Right now, he had no choice but to do as he had been told. Why had Rick given him those sleeping pills? He should never have left Avalon and come back here. It looked as though he was back in his father's clutches again. His father would not listen. He was going to be taken back home and made to marry Cindy. Thanks to Rick, there was now nothing that he could do about it.

There has been no deception. Guinevere's silvery voice filtered through his thoughts. *There was only a desire to protect you. If we had had any doubts over whether your father would listen, you would still be at Avalon. You are not going to return to Boston. You can trust Rick. He merely feared you that you would run blindly into the night and get yourself hurt. We need you to trust us.*

Lance could not be convinced. He felt numb, not knowing what to do or believe. Dazed, he grabbed some clean clothes and shut himself into the bathroom. How could he trust Rick? He had given him no reason to believe that his father would actually listen to him. His father had never listened to anyone in his entire life. How could Rick be so certain that he would listen to him? Even Guinevere's assurances were doing nothing to allay the fears that were gripping him.

Hesitating, Lance let himself out of the bathroom again. Tentatively, he made his way along the hallway and stopped in the living room doorway. His father was here, standing by the window; his hands held behind his back as he stared outside. Rick was here too, standing beside Blake and highlighting how large-framed and well-built Blake Brookes was. He was extremely imposing, and there was no denying that his mere presence demanded respect and unquestioning obedience.

Lance's initial desire was to slip away and flee from the apartment. Rick, however, had noticed him, and as Blake continued to talk, Rick looked directly at Lance. Time seemed to stand still; then Blake eventually realized that Lance was standing in the doorway. Immediately ordering his son into the room, he rummaged in the plastic carrier bag that he was holding.

Lance continued to hover in the doorway, looking round at the front door while his father was distracted. He could escape from the apartment easily enough, but he would then have to make his way down the stairs as he knew he would not have the time to wait for the lift. With no shoes on his feet, however, he would not get far.

Looking back into the room, Lance noticed the way that Rick was watching him. Rick clearly knew what he was thinking. The expression on his face was enough to betray his thoughts. Lance eyed him suspiciously. Rick had deceived him. Yet, through his logical thoughts, Lance could hear Guinevere's voice. He had nothing to fear, and was safe here.

Lance hesitated; then stepped warily into the living room. Melissa was standing in a corner of the room, hidden from view until Lance moved into the room. Not knowing whom to watch, Lance stopped just inside the doorway. He could not trust any of these people. They had all deceived him.

"Ah, here it is." Blake Brookes pulled a disc out of the bag, unaware of the tension and uneasiness in the room. "I'm glad that Rick got this evidence for me. I hate to think what would have happened otherwise. You're not going back to Boston, Lance. What a mess for me to sort out. If that witch thinks she's getting her hands on my company, then she can think again."

Lance remained silent. His mother had joined them and was now escorting him to the kitchen. Distracted once again by the contents of the carrier bag, Lance's father was ignoring them. With no permission given, Mrs Brookes had dared to guide Lance out of the room. A large plate of food was on the table, and Lance stared at it as he stopped just inside the doorway. Still he did not feel hungry, and was not even sure that he wanted any breakfast at all.

Mrs Brookes was still talking, but Lance was unable to hear anything she was saying as he sat at the table. Instead his father's words were spinning around in his head. He was not going back to Boston. He had apparently given his father an enormous problem to sort out. He was clearly ashamed of him and did not want him around any longer. Lance had desperately wanted to stay here; yet now that he had got his wish…

Lance felt numb as he forced a morsel of food down. He could take nothing in, not even Guinevere's calming words. He had dared to face his demons, yet he still had no idea what was going on. He had got what he had wished for, and yet it felt as though he had failed. Once again he had let his father down. He always let his father down.

Unable to eat any more, Lance put his knife and fork down. Beside him in an instant, his mother handed him a mug of coffee as she took the plate away. It was time to return to the living room and face his father again. Lance reluctantly left the sanctuary of the kitchen.

His father was now sitting in the armchair, with Rick and Melissa on the settee. Automatically stopping just inside the doorway, Lance was not yet ready to move any further into the room. His mother, however, was handing round mugs of coffee as she sat beside Melissa.

"I'm flying back home December 27th," Blake Brookes was telling his son, while scanning Lance's laptop before him. "What's all this? What have you been doing, reading about some so-called king and checking our family history? You should have been working."

Mr Brookes deleted everything that Lance had researched. Lance said nothing as he stared at the floor in front of his feet. No-one dared to argue with his father. He had to do everything that his father wanted him to do. Shame and frustration consumed him; Lance crossing over to the window only when he was sure that his father was preoccupied with the laptop. The rain was still falling outside, and Lance stared out towards the distant hills that could not be seen from the apartment. Engrossed in his work, his father had stopped talking. Lance's mother, meanwhile, was flicking through a magazine. Lance was being left alone, and was free to think about other things.

"Are you all right?" Rick asked, suddenly appearing beside him.

Lance gazed steadily at him; then looked away again. After he had been given those sleeping tablets, Lance could not bring himself to trust Rick just yet. He had been deceived, despite Rick having successfully turned his father against Cindy. Now his father had become obsessed with seeking revenge.

Rick was growing increasingly concerned at Lance's lack of response. With his parents here, Rick knew that he could not attempt to discuss anything. That conversation was going to have to wait. Now he was unsure that he had done the right thing, but could do nothing but promise that he would call around again after Lance's father had returned home. Still he got no response, and Rick became increasingly insecure. Right now, though, he had no choice but to join Melissa and leave Lance alone with the very people he did not want to be with. Rick felt as though he had failed, and Blake Brookes was right about one thing. It was all one huge mess.

Chapter 16

Lance had not wanted to get up out of bed this morning. All he had done since his parents had arrived was cough, sneeze and blow his nose. This morning, he had no energy or inclination to do anything, and he felt permanently cold. He wanted to remain hidden beneath the duvet in an attempt to warm himself up once again.

Lance's father, however, had put an abrupt stop to any thoughts of him staying where he was. He wanted his son to travel to the airport with him, where he would board an aeroplane and head back to America. Forced to shower and dress, Lance reluctantly followed his parents down to the waiting car. Shivering, he waited until his mother had climbed into the car before joining her.

"Pull yourself together, Lance," Blake Brookes told him. "It's only a cold, and you've plenty of work to be getting on with."

He climbed into the front of the car, sitting beside Graham as they were driven over to the airport. Lance said nothing, instead resting his head against the window and closing his eyes as he continued to shiver constantly. Whether this was just a cold or not, it was making his head pound. No matter how often he blew his nose, clearing the blockage so that he could breathe more easily had proved impossible.

It was still raining outside, the north wind blowing relentlessly as Graham drove over to the airport. Lance still could not warm up, shivering all the more as he huddled in his coat in the back of the car. Their arrival at the airport came far too quickly, with Lance forced to climb out of the car and into that keen wind and driving rain as ordered by his father. He stepped away from the car, vaguely hearing Graham beginning to object before being abruptly stopped by Lance's father. Whatever Graham had tried to say, it had not stopped Lance listlessly following his parents into the terminal and out of the wind and rain.

Back under shelter, Lance was still finding it an immense effort to summon the energy needed to follow his parents. Time dragged, yet Lance was unaware exactly how much time had actually passed. Sat a short distance from his parents, he had used several tissues before his father at last made his way over to the boarding gate. Lance's mother was in no hurry to leave, instead remaining in the terminal building and watching as the aeroplane that Blake Brookes had boarded accelerated down the rain-soaked runway and rose up into the sky.

At last Lance and his mother were heading back out of the terminal and returning to the car. Mrs Brookes climbed in first, Lance keeping back and waiting for her before climbing in out of the wind and rain himself. Graham was watching him, but Lance remained unaware of him doing so as he huddled into the corner of the car. With his mother flicking through one of the magazines that she had just bought, Lance closed his eyes. There was no conversation as they travelled back to the apartment, and Lance was only made aware of their arrival when he was shaken awake.

He opened his eyes and stared blearily at the face before him. Rick was here, but Lance didn't want to see him, let alone move. He had been completely drained of what energy he had, and wanted to stay right here in the car. Rick hauled him up and out of the car, though, as his mother chastised him for being difficult.

The bitterly cold wind was still blowing, making Lance shiver all the more as they reached the building. Lance did not want the support that he was getting from Rick. He did not want Rick here; he wanted him to leave him alone. They made their way up to the apartment, Lance taking no notice of anything that was going on around them. At last he was allowed to curl up on the settee, ignoring the argument between his mother and Rick. He was too tired to show any interest in anything, except sleeping.

Nancy was furious with Rick for having called for a doctor. Lance was suffering from a cold, and was clearly feeling sorry for himself and making his condition appear worse than it really was. Rick, however, was standing his ground. He believed that the cold was more serious. Lance had not behaved this way before in his short time here. With tempers frayed, the argument stopped only when the doorbell rang.

"Yes, he's got flu," the doctor confirmed, his eyes moving from Rick to Nancy. "Make sure he gets plenty of fluids and as much rest as possible. If he hasn't shaken it off in a week or it gets worse, give me a call."

Nancy Brookes glared at Rick. He had been right after all, and she hated being proved wrong. Blake had claimed that Lance needed to man up, though, and accept that he was suffering from a simple cold. He had been difficult and awkward, and she had shown no patience towards him. She had believed that they were wasting the doctor's time. Instead Rick had been vindicated, and she appeared to be an uncaring mother. Unpleasant as it was to admit, she now knew that Lance should have been left here instead of being dragged to the airport.

The doctor had gone by the time Rick had helped Lance to his bedroom and emerged again. Mrs Brookes was standing in the living room doorway, her arms folded in front of her. The expression on her face was more than enough for Rick to know that she was anything but pleased with him.

"You should have spoken to me, Rick," she told him, "and let me decide what action to take."

"Graham had already tried to raise his concerns." Rick was unrepentant. "But you ignored and rebuked him. He could see how ill Lance is, and tried to tell you. He was so worried that he felt he had no choice but to call me. It looks as though he's been justified too. Surely you're not going to tell me that you prefer to ignore what's right in front of you?"

"Don't you dare judge me when you have no idea what's been going on," Mrs Brookes warned, her voice cold.

"Well, why don't you tell me then? All I know is that Lance had been put in an impossible position. The more I've found out, the more I've wondered how he's not been driven mad. Surely you're not going to tell me that you hadn't noticed how much Cindy Peterson has been manipulating things so that she gets exactly what she wants. Have you not discussed any of this with Lance over these last two days? What kind of life do you think he's had?"

"How can I do that when Blake's been around? He's the head of this family; he's the one in charge. What makes you think he'd let me discuss something like that with Lance? Right now he's preoccupied with how he's going to deal with this. Discussing it with Lance was the last thing on his mind. And what makes you think that you know best? Lance hasn't been particularly keen on having you around, so don't you dare try to criticize me."

Hostility was in Rick's eyes as he gazed at her; then he softened and apologized. Maybe he had been a little hasty, being too wrapped up in his bid to help Lance to notice anything else that was going on. He only wanted to help Lance, to rescue him from the fate that had been waiting for him. He had wanted to do everything he could to prevent the suffering that would have been inevitable.

Lance's mother seemed to relax a little. The intensity of the tension that was in the air faded slightly, neither of them yet ready to back down completely. With Blake flying home, Rick was hoping that he would start to see a difference. To let Mrs Brookes show him that she was capable of caring for her son, Rick needed to take a step back.

He reluctantly left the apartment, unable to argue any longer. It was clear that there was far more that he did not know about the relationship between these three people. There was an awful lot that Lance had obviously not told him. In his desire to get his evidence to Blake Brookes so that he could give Lance the escape route he needed, he had shown no interest in uncovering more information about how this family operated.

Now, as he headed back to his car, he realized that there was far more to this family than he had originally believed.

Rick pulled his car door shut and stared back up at the building. He was questioning whether he had done the right thing, as a nagging doubt swirled in his mind. Was Nancy Brookes really as concerned about her son as she had suggested? There was nothing he could do to answer that question right now. Maybe he should have stayed and coerced Lance's mother into telling him what their lives were really like. Instead, he had backed down and left Lance with the woman who had insisted that he was only suffering from a mere cold.

Rick sighed as he started his engine and headed back towards home. Mrs Brookes had been right about one thing. Ever since Lance's parents had arrived, Lance had not wanted to know Rick. Rick suspected that his parents had said something that had turned Lance against him. With luck it would not be long before Mrs Brookes flew back home too, and maybe then he would be able to find out what was really going on.

Chapter 17

Jerking awake, Lance sat up quickly. Beads of sweat were forming on his skin as he breathed rapidly and heavily. For a moment or two he stared vacantly into space; then he began to look about him. Slowly he calmed down, his breathing returning to normal as he closed his eyes in order to steady his nerves. He had just had another bad dream, his imagination gripping him so fiercely that the visions appeared very real.

Lance rubbed his head; then threw back his duvet and got up onto his feet. He was feeling lightheaded and unsteady on his feet, yet still he grabbed some clean clothes and headed for the bathroom. Washing off all of the sweat and dirt that covered him, he ventured out into the hallway again. Hesitantly, he made his way to the living room doorway and peered into the room.

He was alone in the apartment. Checking every room to be absolutely sure that there was no-one else there with him, he stopped in the kitchen and looked about him. Where was his mother? Lance drank a glass of water; then moved into the living room. Biting his bottom lip, he pondered over the position that he now found himself in, and suddenly made up his mind.

Lance pulled on his trainers and coat and snatched up his wallet and mobile phone; then let himself out of the apartment. He made his way down the stairs, warily checking to see whether anyone was around before slipping out of the building. With his heart beating rapidly and nerves making him tremble, he hurried away along the pavement and stopped outside one of the nearby shops before pulling his mobile phone out of his coat pocket.

Nervously watching the hordes of shoppers streaming past him, Lance eagerly climbed into the taxi he had called for when it pulled up nearby. Now he could relax a little as the car headed away from the city and towards the hills that were on the far side of the valley. It seemed to take a lifetime to reach those hills, but the car continued on until it came to a halt at the bottom of a familiar gorge.

Lance paid the driver; then climbed out of the car and moved back out of the way. A lot of other people were here too, and Lance looked round at them before heading up the road towards the gorge. No-one was taking any notice of him, and Lance was glad to be able to slip away unchallenged. He walked up the hill, passing the cars that were parked on both sides of the narrow road as the sheer rock face rose up behind them.

A cold wind was predictably whistling down through the gorge, making Lance huddle a little further into his coat as he walked purposefully on. He ignored the brown Soay sheep that were wandering freely nearby as he left the black rock behind and moved out onto the open hillside. The wind was blowing more strongly here, the sky blue with a few white clouds scudding by. Having left the people behind, Lance willingly and eagerly moved out into the open and seemingly empty countryside.

Focused entirely upon the place to which he was heading, Lance saw nothing else that was going on around him. There was no-one else around, however, and so no-one could stop him from reaching the wood that was slowly appearing on the distant horizon. He walked on resolutely, stopping only when he had stepped in amongst those trees. Taking a few moments to recover his breath, he moved on once again.

The outermost trees were bare of any leaves, their branches appearing black against the blue-and-white sky. Moving through the wind, Lance could hear the branches rattling against each other. Further into the wood, though, everything had changed. Unseen from the open hillside beyond the wood's boundary, the trees were still covered in leaves, some of them drifting gently to the ground as Lance passed by. There was no wind blowing here; the atmosphere serene as shades of green mingled with the colours of autumn. The coldness of the hills was behind him, the warmth of this part of the wood now filling the air.

Lance headed towards the familiar white light that he could now see ahead of him. Suddenly he was in no immediate hurry, feeling as though he had all the time in the world. The trees eventually opened out into a large clearing, the pale grass stopping at the shores of the lake. A low mist was swirling over the surface of the water, the white light illuminating it eerily as the mist constantly shifted.

A partially hidden island was at the centre of the lake, and Lance gazed across at it as he slowly made his way around the shoreline. Everything was quiet and still; the island the only thing that Lance could see until he approached the spot where he usually stopped. A white rowing boat was floating gently near the bank, and Lance stopped and stared warily at its occupants.

There were three women in the boat. Two of them were dressed in richly coloured velvet robes and cloaks, and sat quietly on either side of the third one who was standing between them. She looked familiar, her long, pale brown hair covering her shoulders and back. She was wearing a pure white dress secured around her slender waist by a silver sash that matched the band that encircled her head.

Lance dared to move a little closer, keeping his eyes upon this third person as he did so. He was concentrating completely upon her, making him unaware of the other people who had come to a stop in the trees behind him.

They had followed him, unnoticed, into the wood, and Rick now stopped Mrs Brookes from stepping out into the clearing. Rick had noticed another woman approaching from a different direction – she looked like the woman who was standing in the rowing boat; Gwyn however wearing a pale yellow dress beneath her green cloak. She too had stopped, and was now resting a hand against a nearby tree as she watched the people in the clearing intently.

Lance had stopped a short distance from where the boat was floating in the water, his eyes firmly upon Guinevere. Smiling quietly and warmly, she offered him a simple wooden cup. Lance looked at it, then back at Guinevere when she urged him to drink the liquid that was inside. It would bring him comfort and help to rid him of the nightmares that had taken hold of him.

As though caught up in some kind of spell, Lance slowly reached out and took the cup from her. He kept his eyes upon her, staring at her for a few long moments that seemed to drag on endlessly before tearing his eyes away and looking down at the cup. The clear liquid that it held was moving gently, just like the black and frigid waters of the lake. Guinevere was encouraging him to drink. That was all that he needed to do.

Staring at the cup as he lifted it up towards his lips, Lance hesitated before looking back at Guinevere. For a fleeting moment, he thought that he had glimpsed very different features. That moment was gone in an instant, though, the queen still smiling as she encouraged him to drink. Doubts suddenly filled Lance's mind. He shook his head slightly, stepped away; then threw the cup as far as he could across the open waters of the lake.

Lance barely noticed the hand and arm that broke free from the surface of the water. Instead he was staring at Guinevere as the hand caught hold of the cup. Then he stepped back out of reach so that the queen could not grab hold of him and drag him into her boat. The hand in the lake held the cup for a moment or two, and then sank back down into the depths and sent ripples extending out across the water's surface as it disappeared from sight.

Lance continued to watch Guinevere as she changed before his very eyes, her face becoming harsh as her hair turned from pale brown to black. Her dress also changed from white to a bright red, a black cloak encasing her velvet robe. The woman screamed with frustration, and the boat suddenly jerked away from the banks of the lake as Lance moved back a little further. The imposter was forced to sit down, the movement of the boat making it impossible for her to stay on her feet.

"I am not the person who you are seeking," Lance called out.

He received no reply, and could only watch as the boat disappeared into the mist before he sat down on the grass and stared out across the still waters of the lake. From her hiding place, Gwyn looked across at Rick and Nancy Brookes; then moved out into the clearing. Sitting beside Lance, she greeted him before congratulating him on passing the first test. Lance said nothing as he continued to stare at the island. Gwyn watched him for a moment or two; then asked him what was bothering him. Lance did not react at first, and then he eventually shrugged his shoulders.

"I have no idea what's going on. Rick tricked me into taking a couple of sleeping tablets so that I was asleep when my parents arrived. When I woke, my father told me that I'm not going back to Boston. He's so ashamed of me that he doesn't want me around any longer. He's got an almighty mess, thanks to me, that he's gone back to sort out. I'd have come here sooner, but I've had the flu. All I've been doing is dreaming the same dream over and over again: that I've been trapped with Cindy and our baby, and from now on she'll be constantly attacking me with nothing I can do to stop it. I was on my own when I woke this morning, so I decided to come here. I didn't expect to be met by Morgan, though, and I don't know why I was given that test."

"I don't think you'll be having any more of those nightmares," Gwyn told him, "not after you broke the spell that Morgan cast over you when you were last here."

Lance looked at her, then behind them as Rick and his mother moved out of the trees and into the clearing. Quick to scramble up onto his feet, he stared warily at them as they made their way across to him. Stopping before him, his mother gazed at him.

"Oh Lance! I've not had the chance to explain everything to you. Your father wanted to concentrate on how best to deal with things, and then you were unwell. I hadn't realized how it must have all sounded to you. Perhaps we should go back home, so I can explain properly."

Lance stared at her' then eventually looked at Gwyn. It was true that he was still not well, and should really be indoors where it was warm. He should be focusing upon building up his strength and at least letting his mother and Rick give him their explanation. Yet he was reluctant – Lance wanted to remain here. There was only one thing that bothered him: these shadows of the past appeared to be convinced that he was the person they were seeking. Though Gwyn had claimed that they did not make mistakes, he had checked his family history more than once. He had no connection with this area, unless he had not yet gone back far enough.

His mother and Rick were still encouraging him to return home. Maybe his priority should be for him to give them the chance to tell him what was going on. Sighing, he gave in for now. Sooner or later, he would return.

Chapter 18

Being the first person to move out of the clearing and back into the trees, Lance was clearly reluctant to leave the lake and its mist-shrouded island. Leaves of many different colours were still drifting to the ground, the trees still retaining their thick canopy despite the number of leaves that were being shed. There was a constant sense of autumn here, as though the final days of this wood were drawing near. The strange white light slowly faded away behind them, the trees becoming devoid of leaves.

Lance stopped upon reaching the edge of the wood and peered out over the open hillside. He was not sure that he wanted to leave this place, and his hesitation betrayed his desire to stay. If he remained here, he could escape from everything that was going on in the outside world. He was going to find nothing out, however, if he chose to remain here. To discover what was going on, he had to leave this sanctuary.

Reluctantly, Lance moved out onto the hillside. With his mother and Rick either side of him, his nervousness increased as his mother began to usher him down the hill. Below them, Rick's car was parked on the roadside, and Lance's mother seemed a little too eager to guide him down to it. Feeling pressured as he was being pushed faster than he wished to go, Lance began to resist his mother's persistence. He did not need to be rushed right now. He needed to be allowed to do this in his own time.

Lance hesitated again, stopping alongside the car. He could sense his mother's impatience, yet he could not stop himself from gazing back up the hill towards the wood that they had just left. Wrapped up in his thoughts, he was blind to the unspoken warning that Rick was giving to Mrs Brookes. He at least was aware that Lance needed to be allowed to do this in his own time, and that they should not rush him for fear of prompting him to flee again.

At last Lance turned away from the hillside and climbed into the car, jumping visibly when Rick quickly slammed the door shut behind him. Mrs Brookes had already climbed into the front passenger seat, and Rick hurried around the car and got behind the wheel. They were heading away, Lance gazing back up the hill and saying nothing as it disappeared from sight.

There was a lot of traffic on the road, the volume increasing as they neared Bristol. Lance was listening to no-one, being too wrapped up in his own thoughts as he imagined that he was elsewhere. Appearing to have no patience with him, Mrs Brookes sighed in frustration as she stared out of the window. They were not that far from the apartment now. Maybe she would be able to talk to him and resolve this issue when they arrived. Maybe then Lance would lose this insane desire to retreat to that wood and they could resume their normal lives.

Rick was determined to join Lance and his mother as they made their way into the modern apartment building. The door closed behind them, shutting out the cold wind that was blowing outside. Stepping into the lift, they watched in silence as the door slid shut before they were suddenly jerked upwards. There was a real tension between them, all of them jumping when Mrs Brookes' mobile phone began to ring. She was quick to pull it out of her pocket, answering the call as the lift stopped moving and the door slid open once more.

Lance followed his mother out into the corridor; then stopped and stared at the two men who were standing by their front door, heavy-looking overcoats covering their suits. The two strangers looked across at the small group before suddenly heading towards them. Introducing themselves as they showed their identification cards, they stared directly at Lance.

Lance could not understand why these two detectives should want to speak to him. They wanted him to go to the police station and tell them about Cindy Peterson there instead of discussing her here. With her telephone conversation abruptly ended, Mrs Brookes objected strongly to them taking Lance away. She wanted them to discuss this here, with her also present.

The detectives remained adamant, and Lance soon found himself with no option but to step back into the lift with the two men. He was wary, remaining silent as they travelled to the police station. Escorted into the building, he was then led into a small interview room and offered one of the chairs that were next to the table.

Lance hesitated; then sat down as he watched the two men move about the room. They were taking off their coats, one of them standing beside the closed door while the other pushed two cassettes into the tape recorder that was on the table before sitting down opposite Lance. Lance stared at the tape recorder, then at the man who was sitting opposite him.

"You're in no trouble," the detective assured him. "We only want your help with our enquiries. I'd like you to tell me about your relationship with Cindy Peterson."

Lance continued to gaze at the detective. He was clearly nervous, and maybe a little frightened. The question had obviously caught him by surprise, and he looked unsure about giving an answer. He looked away and took a deep breath, as though trying to steady his nerves.

"I was supposed to marry her so that our fathers could combine their two companies into one. Now my father has decided that it's not going to happen, and I have no idea why he's changed his mind."

"How about explaining to me how you set Cindy up?" the detective asked.

Quick to look back at him, Lance clearly had no idea what he meant. More questions were asked, Lance growing increasingly confused and agitated with each one. He had no idea what they were suggesting. All that he knew was that he had dared to tell his father that he did not want to marry Cindy, despite being told by her that he had fathered the child that she was expecting.

"I don't know why my father changed his mind. He flew home December 27th, and I've been laid up with the flu ever since. I don't know what's going on. I don't even know what day it is today."

About to speak, the detective instead looked up when there was a knock on the door. He said nothing as his companion took a message that was passed to him to read. Stopping the tapes, he got up and disappeared out of the room.

Lance remained sitting on his chair, staring down at the table as he waited for the detective to return. There was no telling how long this nightmare would continue.

Long minutes passed until Lance looked up at the door when it was opened again. The detective was staring at him, saying nothing as he conceded that maybe Lance was looking pale and tired. He did not want to be reprimanded, though. With Lance gazing at the floor, the detective told him that he was free to leave. Not reacting at first, Lance eventually got up and warily made his way out of the room. He was feeling numb as he was led along the corridor; then ushered through another door before coming face to face with his mother and Rick. Unaware of what was going on around him, he let them guide him back out to the car and back to the apartment.

Sat on the settee, Lance was still feeling numb when his mother handed him something to eat. He had no appetite, despite having not eaten for days. He knew that he had to eat something, though, so that he could start to rebuild his strength. Rick was watching him carefully, waiting until he had eaten what he could before explaining everything to him. Lance listened as best he could, slowly taking in what he had been told before suddenly getting up onto his feet and crossing over to the window.

"You knew three months ago?" he said, daring to look across at Rick at last. "You knew all about this but didn't trust me enough to tell me? You let me carry on believing that I had no way out?"

"I'm sorry. I was waiting for the appropriate moment."

"No, Rick. You expected me to tell you everything, yet you could not do the same. And what's more, you preferred to give me some tablets to make me sleep, just so that you didn't have to tell me."

"I didn't know whether you'd be able to cope with knowing. Maybe I should have told you, but you had plucked up the courage to stand up to your father without knowing about this. And you have just shown those two policemen that you really did not know what's been going on."

Lance turned away and stared out of the window. Rick's excuses sounded weak. Lance knew that it would have been much easier for him to confront his father if he had known about Cindy's confession. He would never have felt obliged to speak to her first if he had known. Now he was really struggling to take everything in. His father had seen the evidence and had taken a copy of the footage back to America to confront the Petersons. He was not about to let them take everything that he had built up from nothing. Lance slowly realized that Cindy now had no hold over him, unless she succeeded in convincing everyone that her confession had been staged.

Still, Rick had obviously not trusted Lance enough to tell him about Cindy's confession. This could all have been resolved three months ago. Instead, he had been left to believe that he had no way out. Right now, he was not sure that he could forgive Rick for keeping this from him. They still had to prove that he had not brought in an actress who looked like Cindy to say all of the things that had been said on the DVD that Lance had not yet seen. No wonder his father had called it an enormous mess. No doubt the possibility of him losing everything because of this was very real. Now Lance was beginning to understand why his father had not wanted him to return to Boston. This time, he had messed up in a major way.

Chapter 19

Parking at the side of the road, Lance looked up at the cluster of familiar trees before starting to climb the hillside. The knowledge that Graham would call Rick as soon as he left with the car was spurring him to move quickly. He had made no secret of his desire to come here, and knowing that, Rick would most likely come to this wood in search of him. There had been no point in trying to hide his true intention. The only thing that was on his mind right now was his wish to spend as much time as he could here before being joined by Rick and his mother.

Lance barely hesitated when he reached the trees. He did not stop or glance round to see whether he had been followed before moving into the shelter of the wood. He was focusing upon reaching the one place where he wanted to be, the one place where he felt that he could relax. His surroundings quickly softened as he walked on and started to pass between trees that were still holding onto their leaves.

A white light pierced through the trees ahead of him, and Lance headed directly towards it until he stepped out into the familiar clearing.

The water of the nearby lake was calm and still, its black depths looking cold and uninviting. Lance moved on, skirting around the frigid water before stopping close to the bank. Staring across at the island for a few minutes, he then sat down on the grass.

He was completely unaware of the people who were closing in on him through the trees; instead focusing entirely on the island in the lake. Behind him, Rick had snatched hold of Mrs Brookes' arm to prevent her from moving out into the clearing. Again he had noticed Gwyn approaching, and he knew that Lance would talk to her. He and Lance's mother would learn so much more as long as they remained hidden among the trees.

Gwyn moved forwards into the clearing. She was acutely aware of the presence of the other two. She had received no warning from Guinevere, though, the queen instead urging her on. Silently walking across to where Lance was sitting, she noted how he quickly looked up at her when she stopped and sat down beside him. He was looking across at the island again, both of them already feeling comfortable in each other's company. Lance could relax in the knowledge that she would not judge him on his words or actions. Gwyn would say nothing, and because of that Lance was able to confess to many thoughts and fears.

"Is anything wrong?" Gwyn asked, breaking the tranquil silence.

Lance continued to gaze across at the island as he absentmindedly toyed with the car keys that were in his hand. They were sitting a short distance from the shores of the lake, the white light illuminating everything around them. Silence had returned, but Gwyn remained calm despite getting no answer.

"I don't believe that Morgan will come for you today," she said.

"I'm not waiting for Morgan," Lance responded, refusing to look at her. "I've come to think; nothing more."

Gwyn smiled kindly. She remained as acutely aware of the two people who were hiding among the nearby trees as Lance was oblivious of their presence. He appeared interested only in Avalon, his gaze firmly remaining upon that island.

"So what is wrong?" Gwyn asked again.

Lance momentarily glanced round at her before shaking his head as though not wanting to speak. Almost immediately, though, he began to talk.

"I really don't understand what's going on," he confessed. "Apparently Rick's gathered some proof of what the Petersons had planned to do, and now I'm being accused of setting Cindy up."

"I don't believe for a moment that you would even consider doing such a thing. What's going to happen?"

Gwyn waited patiently while Lance hesitated before continuing. His father was fighting the

169

allegation. His lawyers had wanted to confiscate the laptops belonging to Cindy and a man in Boston called Phil Jameson, who was a well-known drug dealer. Those laptops should have been seized by now, but they would need time to retrieve the information they were seeking. All that he could do for now was wait, and if they found nothing, then it looked as though he was going to be in serious trouble.

"They'll find what they're looking for." Gwyn sounded confident.

"I know," Lance agreed.

Gwyn was momentarily lost for words as she glanced at him, and then she asked him what could possibly be worrying him enough to bring him here. Lance looked at her properly for a moment or two, before becoming unable to hold her gaze. He had to look away again and stare at the ground as he explained. He feared that his father would not believe him. He was only too aware of how persuasive Cindy could be, and he feared that his father would believe her claims and turn against him once again. After all, he had told his father that he hated him.

He had not really meant what he had said. He simply hated the way that his father had complete control over his whole life. The reality was that he also admired his father, no matter how much he did hate him. He could always sort out any major problem as though it was just a trivial inconvenience. He thought nothing of tackling the big guns. By rights, his father was the one who should hate *him*: he had only ever let him down. So much was being expected of him as his father looked to him to judge whether he was worthy enough to inherit the empire that he had spent his lifetime building up from nothing. All that Lance ever seemed to do, though, was mess things up. He had to be such a disappointment, such an embarrassment. Look at him right now: what had he done when faced with a problem that needed solving? He had done what he had always done. He had run away, just like the coward that he really was.

"You've just told me that you came here to think." Gwyn smiled quietly. "And that is something that you obviously find easier to do when here. You are no coward."

Again Lance shook his head as he insisted that he had shown how feeble he was by running away. He did not deserve his father's help, and he certainly did not deserve to be allowed so close to someone as heroic and noble as King Arthur.

He was no coward, Gwyn repeated. He was facing up to his fears and was, in his own quiet way, showing the courage that he did have. He did not have to stand up to giants like his father to show his bravery. He did not have to wield a sword to complete heroic acts like King Arthur. He was showing a different kind of courage. Very few people could resist Morgan. Most would have readily accepted that chalice from her. They would have fallen at the first hurdle and left this world, never to return. There would have been no going to Avalon. Only the most noble and courageous were allowed to go there. He had shown Morgan that he was much stronger than she had believed.

Lance was on the verge of looking at her when he caught sight of a shining object that was lying on the grass between them and the shore of the lake. Getting up onto his feet, he moved forwards and picked it up. It was a dagger, its silver blade glinting brightly in the white light. The hilt was studded with an array of jewels of many colours, and Lance was transfixed as each and every one reflected the white light that was shining down upon him.

He became aware of a voice drifting on the light breeze, promising him a life of perpetual peace and happiness instead of this life of pain and torment. Lance wrapped his fingers around the jewel-studded handle. Everything else around him dissolved as Lance stared at the dagger. He was alone with this weapon and the promise of a better life. There was no denying that the offer to escape from his nightmare existence was very tempting.

Lance's mouth suddenly hardened and tightened as he gripped the handle a little more tightly. He could sense a rowing boat starting its journey towards him across the lake. Someone was heading towards him, and Lance suddenly felt threatened. Forcing himself out of the trance that he had fallen under, he hurled the dagger as far as he could over the surface of the lake. With his eyes fixed upon it as it cut a path through the air, he watched as the knife turned over and over.

Without warning, a hand appeared from nowhere. Droplets of water fell back into the lake as the hand reached up, fingers quickly wrapping around the jewel-studded hilt, the blade glinting brightly as it was pointed skywards. Lance watched as it was held still for a few long moments, the blade lengthening considerably as the dagger was slowly lowered into the still waters of the lake and disappeared from view.

Ripples extended across the surface of the lake as Lance continued to stare across the water. Those ripples were the only proof that he had not dreamt what had happened. A familiar boat was out there, hidden by the swirling mists, and Lance could picture three women on board. Morgan, it appeared, had been coming for him after all. She had been the person who had sent him that dagger, and she had been the one who had whispered all of those false promises. She had wanted him to use it to stab himself, but instead he had hurled it into the lake and watched as it had regained its true form. The Lady of the Lake had reached up and snatched it before Morgan could claim it back. The enchantress would undoubtedly be far from pleased now. She had failed for a second time. He was not as weak and gullible as she had believed, and now there was nothing that she could do to stop the water nymphs from steering her away from this shore.

Lance shuddered a little; then suddenly realized that Gwyn was standing beside him. She was saying nothing as she smiled. Words were not needed. Lance knew exactly what he had just done, even if he was not quite ready to believe in it just yet. They stood in silence, the sound of a nearby telephone ringing shrilly stopping Lance from speaking before he had the chance to say a single word. Quickly looking round, he was at last aware of the presence of his mother and Rick.

Lance watched his mother as she answered her mobile phone. He had completely forgotten that he would inevitably have been followed here. He had not given his mother and Rick a second thought while he had been sitting here and talking to Gwyn. Now he could do nothing but listen to his mother's side of her conversation, and when his father's name was uttered, he knew who she was talking to. There was nothing else that he could do but wait until the call had ended, his mother staring at her phone as she switched it off before glancing at Rick and then looking across at Lance.

"Cindy was at Phil's apartment when the police called for his laptop," she informed him, "and she was far from happy at being caught there with him. She's admitted that they were only ever interested in getting hold of your father's company so that they could eliminate the only competition they have."

Mrs Brookes hesitated, now preferring to look back at Rick. Cindy had claimed that their conversations had only been a bit of idle fun. They had had no intention of carrying out any of their suggestions. Lance was in the clear, and Mrs Brookes turning back to face him once more. Cindy, however, was still claiming that he was the father of the baby that she was expecting.

"Why can't she just let it go?" Lance sounded exasperated.

"There's really no need for you to worry, Lance. She's clinging onto the last thing that she thinks she can. She's lost all of her credibility though, and she's not going to be believed by anyone after all of the lies that she's told. Even her gynaecologist has pointed out that her dates are all wrong for you to be the father. You were over here at the time, so you can't possibly be the father, no matter how much Cindy insists that you are."

Mrs Brookes crossed over to where he was standing and told him that everything was going to be all right. With his father in charge, Lance knew that it would be.

"I heard what you said just now," she confessed, "and I don't believe that your father will believe anything that the Petersons might say now."

She turned again, this time looking at Gwyn as she invited her for a coffee so that she could be thanked properly for what she had done. Gwyn smiled sadly as she shook her head. She could not accept the kind offer that had been made. She was misunderstood, and was only tolerated because she kept out of everyone's way. She could, however, invite them into her home if they wanted to have a coffee with her.

Rick handed the car keys over to Lance's mother before speaking. Claiming that he had work to do, he was not stopped by Lance or Mrs Brookes as he disappeared through the trees. Instead, they followed Gwyn away from the lake and into the trees. The white light gradually faded away behind them and at last Lance was about to see where Gwyn lived. With a sense of anticipation, he willingly followed her. His memories remained bright and clear despite the light fading behind him, and right now, he could only focus upon discovering what kind of castle Gwyn lived in.

Chapter 20

Grey slate tiles covered the roof of the small house that stood just outside the boundary of the wood. With a small window on each side of a solid wooden door, the building appeared harsh and uninviting. Lance and his mother both stopped in surprise when they emerged from the trees. Just like the weather, the house looked hostile and cold.

Gwyn did not hesitate, and continued on, crossing first a narrow strip of open hillside and then an unmade track before finally stopping by the simple garden gate that was set in the stone wall. She patiently waited for them to join her, holding the gate open for them before moving on once again. A flagstone path contrasted harshly with turf that was cropped short by wild rabbits, and Lance again moved warily forwards in the direction of the solid wooden door.

That door was never locked. With the house hidden from sight by the contours of the earth, no-one ever stumbled across it as they ventured over the hills. Gwyn opened the door and stepped inside before disappearing along a dark hallway and through a doorway to her right. Her companions followed, Lance looking about him as he walked behind his mother. He had expected a castle. Instead, Gwyn had brought them to a hovel.

Gwyn had already filled an old kettle with water and was placing it on top of the Aga when Lance and his mother joined her in her little kitchen. They could only look about them in disbelief. It all looked so old and dated. Well-used furniture was standing on the flagstone floor, while cheap and tacky cupboards stretched along the length of one of the walls. An old sink stood against the window, beside which was an ancient fridge. No words could describe what they were now seeing. The silence was broken when Gwyn suggested that they sat at the table that was in the middle of the room.

Finally moving away from the door, they crossed the short distance to the table and sat down as Gwyn set mugs of coffee before them. Then she turned and picked up a third mug before joining them. Almost immediately Mrs Brookes broke the silence. Having always seemed to know what to say, she now wanted to know everything about Gwyn and why she had chosen to live this kind of life.

As Mrs Brookes asked Gwyn a multitude of questions, Lance began to look about the room again. Everything really did appear to be old, and it looked as though it had been brought in from somewhere else after it had finished its useful life and then been forced to fit into this room. It was obvious that Gwyn had nothing that was of any value. The squalor that she was living in shocked him; yet she was so happy and contented with her life as she appreciated even the smallest and most insignificant thing that came her way. Compared to this, he lived a life of luxury and opulence.

Lance looked back round when his mother moved. She had reached forwards and was now picking up the partly-finished embroidery that was lying on the table. Curiosity had taken hold, Mrs Brookes immediately losing all interest in her conversation with Gwyn as she inspected the picture that was in the process of being revealed on the piece of fabric.

"I had no idea that you did this sort of thing," she remarked, not seeing the way that Gwyn had glanced across at Lance.

"It's a new design that I'm working on at the moment," Gwyn informed her. "That's what I do to earn a living: I design, like my mum used to. I draw the picture, choose the colours and then stitch to see how it turns out. Gareth sells my designs in our shop in Glastonbury. Mum and I used to work together before she died. I'm just carrying on from where she left off."

"Really? How quaint. I'd love to see all of your creations, both yours and your mother's."

Gwyn looked reluctant and embarrassed as she got up and left the room. Long moments passed, Gwyn sensing how uncomfortable Lance was feeling when she returned with a small cardboard box. Mrs Brookes was already emptying the box as Gwyn sat back down. Pulling out every piece of embroidery that was inside, she held them up so that she could look at them. Each and every one was intricate and delicate, small pieces of treasure that to Gwyn were priceless.

Upon hearing Mrs Brookes' suggestion that the designs must sell well, Gwyn surprised her by shrugging her shoulders. Gareth was the one who was in the shop doing the selling. She had no idea how many, if any, were sold. She stayed here, well away from the shop, and spent her time creating new designs for Gareth to sell. Here was where she felt most inspired, and this was where she truly wanted to be. Here was where she felt most connected to the world of King Arthur.

Mrs Brookes was gazing admiringly at the piece of embroidery that she was holding up so that the daylight shone through it. She was smiling, the corners of her eyes creasing. She appeared wistful, and then her expression changed as she looked across at Gwyn.

"You'd sell loads back at home, back in New England," she stated, "I'm sure of it. They'd go down a storm over there. This is the kind of thing that people adore. I'd like to open a shop in Boston; sell them over there for you."

"I don't know." Gwyn looked taken aback. "Gareth deals with the selling. I'll have to see what he says."

They heard the sound of a car approaching on the unmade track, and stopping outside. Someone appeared in the doorway, and Lance recognized him immediately. In turn, Gareth stared back at Lance and his mother, as he demanded to know what was going on. The hostility that was in his voice was clear, but Gwyn chose to ignore it as she moved the kettle back onto the Aga.

"We're having a coffee," she told him. "Mrs Brookes would like to open a shop in America so she can sell our embroideries there."

Gareth had been staring menacingly at Lance and his mother. Now he looked across at his sister, then back at Mrs Brookes. She wanted to sell their designs in America? As though unaware of the hostility, Mrs Brookes sounded enthusiastic as she suggested that they meet up that afternoon to discuss the possibility properly. Gareth still sounded hostile as he reluctantly agreed.

"I'll be at the shop in Glastonbury, he stated. "Just round the corner from the entrance to the Abbey."

Mrs Brookes smiled politely as she got to her feet. It was time for her and Lance to return to Bristol. Crossing over to the door, she thanked Gwyn for the coffee; then looked back at Lance. He had felt more than a little uncomfortable since

Gareth had arrived, and now he willingly followed his mother outside and pulled the door shut behind them, cursing silently to himself. Yet again he had run away from confrontation. Shutting the gate, Lance and his mother stared in surprise at the new car that was parked on the track.

Lance's mind was elsewhere as he entered the wood and passed the lake. Something was not right. While Gwyn was living in poverty, her brother was driving around in a brand new car. Gwyn, however, would never hear a bad word against Gareth, and Lance knew that she would refuse to acknowledge how unfair it appeared to other people. He would not be able to say anything to her, knowing that he would jeopardize their friendship if he tried.

They had emerged out onto the open hillside again before Lance realized that they had passed the lake. He had been too absorbed in his thoughts to notice. Now his mother was ushering him down the hill, the grass wet and slippery beneath their feet. It had stopped raining, the dark grey clouds having been driven across the sky by the strong wind. His silence went unnoticed by his mother as she talked continually. Totally absorbed in the excitement of her proposal, she was already making plans for her new venture.

Mrs Brookes suddenly stopped and looked round at Lance when they reached the car. Everything, she assured him, was going to be all right. His father was going to make sure that the Petersons would not get away with their lies and accusations. He was determined to make sure that they paid for what they had tried to do.

"I know." Lance spoke quietly. "Mom, I just needed to get away from the office this morning. I really did only come here so I could think, nothing more."

Mrs Brookes smiled sadly, her expression betraying her doubts as she unlocked the car. She was glad to get out of the keen wind that was blowing, and determined to drive back to the office despite the almost inevitable struggle to handle a car that she had never been in before.

Lance reluctantly followed his mother to a nearby café for lunch once they were back in Bristol. He was too preoccupied with his memories of the dagger to want to talk. What had made him hurl it back into the lake, he did not know. He could not explain his actions. It had simply felt like the right thing to do. Seeing that hand break free from the water and catch hold of it had not surprised him at all, though. If anything, he had expected it to happen. Of one thing he was certain: he had made the right choice. He had passed the second test. Yet he still could not understand why those ghosts of people from the past continued to believe that he was the person they were seeking.

Mrs Brookes barely watched Lance as he made his way up to the office after lunch. She was keen to go to Glastonbury; to climb into the back of the chauffeured car and pull out her mobile phone as they joined the Bristol traffic. Now out of Lance's earshot, she was at last able to call her husband and tell him everything.

"I'm not sure that he does want to return home if it means working with you, Blake." Mrs Brookes paused for the briefest of moments. "Maybe he'll consider working with me in the shop that I want to open. I'm going to sell embroideries."

"Embroideries?" Blake Brookes questioned.

"Yes, embroideries," Mrs Brookes confirmed. "Gwyn designs them and her brother sells them. I'm actually on my way to discuss the prospect of me selling them in Boston."

"Embroideries?" Mr Brookes repeated, his disdain clearly audible in his voice.

"It's a popular pastime, Blake. I know that they'll sell well, and I know they're not logical, but that doesn't mean that they can't be a lucrative business. Anyway, how are you getting on over there?"

Mr Brookes was getting on very well. He was determined to make sure that the Petersons would pay for what they had planned to do. He was not going to let them take his company from him. He was not going to let them take everything that he had worked so hard to build up. He was going to make sure that everyone found out what they had planned to do, right down to the smallest detail. In fact, he was going to call Lance right now and tell him what he was doing.

The line went dead, Mrs Brookes and stared at her phone before switching it off. Her husband would already be talking to Lance before she had the chance to call Blake again. Mrs Brookes sighed with frustration; then turned her attention to her imminent meeting with Gareth. That was what she needed to concentrate on. Right now, nothing else mattered.

Chapter 21

Mrs Brookes gazed about her as she walked into the shop. She was in a real Aladdin's cave; surrounded by an exquisite treasure trove. With the young shop assistant busy with some customers, Mrs Brookes had plenty of time in which to have a good look around her. She recognized a lot of the designs, having seen the original pieces of work only that morning. At last the shop assistant approached her, making her look round. She had come to see Gareth, she explained. She then watched in silence as the assistant disappeared through a door at the back of the shop.

It had been obvious that the shop assistant had been told nothing of Mrs Brookes' visit. Not impressed, Mrs Brookes nonetheless decided to say nothing as two more people entered the shop. The shop, she had been told, was always busy as they sold to an eager public. Gareth's new car only confirmed how successful this business truly was, and yet Gwyn was living in a hovel. None of this made any sense.

Mrs Brookes looked round when Gareth called out her name. She hesitated for the briefest of moments as she glanced across at the shop assistant, and then she moved into the office that was behind the shop. Offered a chair, she appeared completely at ease as she watched Gareth sit down in the chair across the desk. He had not expected her to actually come over, and had been caught by surprise at her arrival. That she was actually serious about wanting to sell their designs in America was unbelievable.

"I would not be here if I was not serious," Mrs Brookes remarked. "I do not believe in wasting my time. You appear to be doing very well, though I'm shocked to see your sister living with very little."

"That is how my sister chooses to live," Gareth stated quickly, sounding defensive. "She doesn't want to live in any other way. You do realize that my sister lives in a complete fantasy world?"

Mrs Brookes eyed him suspiciously. "I'm not so sure about that. Does Gwyn actually know how well you're doing?"

"She has no interest in this shop. She prefers to keep herself to herself, and I would do anything to protect her. She asks for only the materials that she needs to produce new designs, and I'm more than happy to oblige. What does she think of your proposal?"

"She didn't get a chance to say before you turned up. She only had time to tell me that you deal with sales. I am no fool, though. If I do not like any agreement that is drawn up, then there will be no deal. It is only a proposal at the moment. I have no idea how lucrative the American market might be. I do want to see your latest set of accounts though, so I can see what kind of figures I could be looking at."

She left holding a catalogue and climbed into the back of the car. The street was narrow and busy, and on either side there was a mishmash of shop after shop filled with supernatural-themed goods. They appeared to be squashed together, fighting each other not only for space, but also for trade. Mrs Brookes, however, continued to stare at the one shop that she had just visited. She had never met anyone as obnoxious as Gareth Mortimer. Sure that he was hiding something, she could think of no other reason why he should refuse to show her his accounts. She was convinced that there was something very unsavoury going on. Gareth had claimed to care about his sister, and yet he was happy to let her live in poverty.

Mrs Brookes continued to stare at the shop as Graham pulled out of the parking space. The shop slipped quickly out of sight as they moved up the road and headed back to Bristol. Eventually she turned her attention to the catalogue, her mind racing as she looked through it. She was not beaten yet, not by a long shot. She needed to talk to people back in Boston. She needed to do a proper investigation. She needed to compile some facts and figures.

Lance was sitting at his desk with the computer screen in front of him, the sudden shrill ringing of the telephone making him stare at it warily. With Rick sitting beside him, Lance knew instinctively that it was his father on the other end. Swallowing, he reached across and answered the call. He could only stare blankly ahead while his father spoke. Not once was he asked for his opinion. Instead, he was expected to meekly agree with everything that his father was saying. What else could he do? His father had always bulldozed ahead and done whatever he wanted to do. Whatever Lance thought or felt was irrelevant. That did not even come into consideration.

The line suddenly went dead, Lance swallowing as he slowly replaced the receiver and continued to stare into space. Rick eventually broke the tense silence, Lance quickly snapping out of his trance as he looked round at him. Rick had said nothing as he had listened to Lance talking to his father. Now, though, he was asking him if he wanted to return to Avalon.

Lance shook his head. He did not need to return just yet. There was nothing that he needed to think about right now. Lance sat for a moment or two longer; then began to explain what had been said. His father was going to press charges. He wanted everyone to know what the Petersons had planned to do. He wanted everyone to know how they had planned to take everything that he had worked so hard for, and he wanted everyone to know that that was why he had called off his son's wedding to their daughter. He wanted everyone to know what kind of people they really were.

"He doesn't need to reveal everything," Rick said.

"Oh, he does," Lance answered, a little too quickly as he got up and crossed over to the window. "Of course he needs to reveal everything, right down to the tiniest detail. He'll be after every last thing they own in compensation for what they planned to take from him."

Lance stared outside. He knew that, soon, everyone but him would know what the Petersons had planned to do. He could sense Rick stopping alongside him, the tense silence broken by Rick urging him to talk to his mother. Lance glanced at him before quickly looking away again. He knew that talking to his mother would be a complete waste of time. His father was hungry for revenge, and determined to reveal absolutely everything. Nothing that anyone might say would make any difference. There would be no point in talking to his mother. There would be no point in talking to anyone. His father was not going to change his mind.

"I succeeded," Rick pointed out, "and you stood up to your father."

Lance glanced fleetingly at him again. Rick urged him once more to talk to his mother. Lance was not convinced that it couldn't do any harm. He couldn't see how anyone, even his mother, could reason with his father. Besides, he could not see his mother being interested when she returned from Glastonbury. Only when reunited with her would they know.

Mrs Brookes made her way up to the office once back in Bristol, finding Lance and Rick sitting in front of the computer screen. Rick was explaining something, and Lance was actually showing a glimmer of interest. Mrs Brookes had already pulled a notebook out of her bag, and now she retrieved a telephone number from it and picked up the phone. Looking at each other, Lance and Rick said nothing. Mrs Brookes was too engrossed in what she was doing to take any notice of them; making telephone calls and sending images from the catalogue.

Rick led Lance out of the room when they were eventually pushed away from the computer. Sitting at a table in the canteen, Lance gazed vacantly down at the tabletop while Rick fetched two cardboard cups of coffee. He had retreated into himself again, once more shutting himself off from the rest of the world. All that Rick could do was urge him again to talk to his mother.

Lance asked how he was supposed to do that. Surely Rick had noticed that his mother was only interested in one thing at the moment? Lance gazed defiantly at him, and then looked back down at his cardboard cup. The observation was one that Rick could not argue with. He had seen what Mrs Brookes had been like when she returned, and her enthusiasm for her new project rivalled her husband's for his computers.

Rick suddenly realized what was going on. Lance was stuck in the middle, trapped between two people who were too wrapped up in their own worlds to notice that he actually existed. He might just as well not be here. Incensed, Rick could not stop himself from blurting out his thoughts. His whole life had always been like this, hadn't it? Neither of his parents had ever shown any interest in him.

Lance held his gaze for a few long moments before looking away again. What his life had been like, and what it continued to be like, was nothing to do with Rick. So what if his parents ignored him? They had produced their son and heir. He had proved to be nothing but a huge disappointment to them though, and had not turned out to be the person his father had desired.

In response, Rick said that he did not believe that Lance's father looked upon him as a disappointment, especially after everything that had happened lately. Lance sighed. Rick had no idea how well respected the Petersons were. He had been the lucky one when he was engaged to

Cindy. He had had it all. His father owned a highly successful company which he was to inherit, and he had a beautiful fiancée whose father was richer and more successful than his own. How could he have not been the luckiest man on the planet? Only he had thrown it all away, and now the two fathers were at each other's throats. He had messed up big time.

"You have not messed up, Lance," Rick insisted. "If you knew what Cindy planned to do to you, if everyone knew, then no-one would want to know them."

"Which is exactly why my father has to bring it all out into the open. It's why he's taking them to court, so that everyone *does* know. It's the only way that he can protect the company and himself."

Lance was looking directly at Rick, his outburst quickly coming to an abrupt end. He had betrayed his father enough with what he had just said. Ready to return to the office, Lance got to his feet. Stopping him, Rick insisted that he went down to Graham instead while he fetched his mother.

Rick watched Lance walk away. His shoulders were hunched and his eyes fixed upon the floor as he headed towards the stairs. Anger rose up inside Rick, and he waited until Lance had disappeared from sight before he made his way back to the office. Mrs Brookes was still busy, her eyes fixed upon the computer screen as Rick watched her for a moment or two.

"Could I have a quick word?" he asked.

"In a minute." Mrs Brookes' eyes remained firmly upon the screen before her.

"I don't know that it can wait." Rick sounded annoyed and angry. "Have you really not noticed that your son is not here? Don't you know that his father called him earlier to tell him that he's pressing charges against the Petersons?"

Mrs Brookes cursed loudly as she immediately abandoned the computer and bundled her paperwork into her bag before hurrying out of the room. Rick said nothing as he watched her go. What could he say? Lance would not want to discuss anything now, and yet he needed to talk. Only time would reveal whether he would do just that.

Chapter 22

"What do you want from them, Lance?"

Lance was feeling numb as he held the telephone receiver to his ear. His father's question had caught him off-guard, Mr Brookes asking the question again as he demanded an answer.

"Just for them to leave me alone," Lance answered, his voice quiet and timid, "and for me to never to see any of them again, particularly Cindy."

"Oh, you'll want more than that. Leave it with me. I'll make sure that you get no less than what you deserve."

The call was ended, and Lance was left staring into space as he sat in silence in front of the desk. The conversation that he had just had with his father was the same as the one he had had with his mother the previous afternoon. He had not said much to her, either.

Lance had been leaning against the car when his mother burst out of the building and hurried across to where he was waiting. He had turned away when she approached, and climbed into the back of the car after her. Nothing had been said as they travelled back to the apartment, where he told her what he had just told his father. He simply wanted the Petersons to disappear out of his life.

Lance snapped out of his trance upon realizing that Rick was speaking to him. He was not concentrating on work. With everything that was going on, this was no surprise. There was no point in continuing just yet, so Rick suggested that they got something to eat. Lance hesitated; then got up and grabbed his coat. Maybe he should escape for a while.

The pair pulled on their coats as they made their way across the foyer and let themselves out through the glass door. A bitterly cold wind was blowing outside; the significant drop in temperature overnight catching everyone by surprise. That wind was now buffeting the pair as they made their way along the rain-soaked pavement. Black clouds hung ominously overhead, blotting out much of the natural light as more rain threatened to fall.

Rick and Lance gladly stepped into the shelter of a nearby café. Sitting at a table in a quiet corner away from the window, they ordered coffee and something to eat. It was still relatively quiet, the lunchtime rush not yet started. It would have been early morning in Boston when Blake Brookes had called his son, and he would now undoubtedly be getting ready to make the short journey to his office. He would have called from the Boston apartment, which was conveniently sited close to his office building.

Lance looked up only when the waitress put two mugs of coffee down on the table. Mumbling his thanks, he stared at the mug that was now before him. Rick watched the waitress as she began to move away. Stirring sugar into his coffee, he kept his eyes upon his mug as he spoke.

"Will your mother be joining us this afternoon?" he asked.

"I don't know." Lance shrugged his shoulders. "I have no idea what Mom has planned to do."

"You did actually talk to her yesterday, didn't you?" Rick eyed him suspiciously.

Lance glanced across at him, but was unable to hold his gaze. Rick wanted an answer, and he was clearly not going to drop the subject until he got one.

Lance stared at his mug of coffee as he carefully considered what answer he was going to give. His mother had wanted to know what it was that he wanted, and he could only give her the same answer that he had given to his father. He knew that there was no guarantee that he would be left alone by the Petersons, just as there was no guarantee that he had not fathered the baby that Cindy was expecting. Her gynaecologist had, after all, simply said that it was highly improbable. The possibility had by no means been ruled out.

Cindy Peterson was still insisting that he was the father, despite having been shown the evidence that she had claimed otherwise. She had been telling so many lies lately, though, that there was no telling what the truth was. Lance knew that the only way of putting a stop to all of this was to let his father take the Petersons to court. It all made him feel uncertain about whether he wanted to return home instead of remaining here. He feared the Bostonians' reaction to his father taking on the Petersons, and yet he also feared the real possibility of never being able to return home.

"Well I for one won't be sorry if you decide to stay here with us," Rick remarked, making Lance look up at him. "I know that we didn't get on at all when you first joined us. But now, well... things just won't be the same without you around. Have you given any thought to what it would be like if you decided to settle here?"

There was a hint of a smile on Lance's face. He saw no point in even considering such a thing. The harsh reality was that come next summer, he would be flying back to Boston and would not be coming back. By then, his father was expecting him to have learned and understood every aspect of this branch. It would be pointless for him to contemplate any other scenario. All that he could do was to make the most of the time that he had here while he still could.

Rick could not understand why Lance's mother couldn't say something on his behalf. Had even told her? Lance hesitated before nodding. He had told his mother that he was not sure that he wanted to leave England, yes, however she had asked whether it was in fact Avalon that he did not want to leave. That question was one he was still unable to answer, and it was all irrelevant anyway. That choice was not his to make. There was nothing that anyone could say, and if his mother had tried, his father had not mentioned it. Maybe, Lance suggested, she would say something when she returned home in a couple of days.

"Your mother is going back home?" Rick sounded genuinely surprised.

"Yes. She wants to get things moving with the new project she's planning. She's done everything that she possibly can from here, and can't do anything else until she's back in Boston. There's no point in her staying here with me any longer, and there's nothing more that she can do to help me."

"But Lance, she's your mother. She's supposed to support you."

"I've not had a normal upbringing, if you haven't realized that already. My mother was hardly ever around. I was raised by people who were paid by my father to teach me about nothing but computers. If Mom had been around, then she wouldn't have been allowed to have any involvement with me anyway. I'm not used to her being around. I think I'd actually prefer it if she'd return home and leave me in peace."

Lance fell silent again, eventually looking across at Rick as he got no response. Rick was staring at him in disbelief, as though he was unable to take in what he had just been told. Yet again Lance quickly looked away. Rick needed to remember that Blake Brookes was a very dominant person. He demanded respect and obedience from everyone around him. Years ago, Lance had overheard his father telling his mother that he was to do nothing but learn about his computers. It was the only thing that he was to be allowed to live and breathe, and was to be his entire life. Rick already knew that no-one was ever allowed to argue with Lance's father, and why should he treat his wife and son any differently? Saying something to Blake would be pointless – he would not listen. At least Lance's mother could escape for a while and pretend that none of this was happening. Lance was not going to deny her that luxury. He was not going to ask her to stay or force her to live a miserable life. He could not be that unfair.

"Then we'll do it, Lance," Rick said, pausing as the waitress brought them their meals. "If you want to stay here, we'll set up on our own."

Lance shook his head. It was a nice thought, which left him feeling flattered, but they had no money and would never be able to secure the

200

financial support they would need. Then there was the fact that his father would come straight over. They both knew that Rick would be sacked immediately and Lance would be dragged back to Boston. And even if, by some miracle, they did manage to set up on their own, Mr Brookes would crush them before they could even begin to trade. He was not worth Rick losing everything for. For everyone else's sake, Lance would do as his father wished and return home next summer, never to come back.

"There is something that I'll be taking back with me." Lance stopped Rick when he began to object. "Something that even my father will not be able to take away from me. I'll have a whole load of memories of everyone here. I know that I didn't want to get to know anyone at first, but you'll stay with me for the rest of my life. In my mind I'll always be able to escape back here, and there's nothing that my father will be able to do to stop it."

Rick shook his head sadly. There had to be something they could do. Had Blake Brookes learned nothing? There was nothing more that could be said right now. Lance more than anyone knew what his own father was like. They could do nothing but eat their meals as the café began to fill with people, and when it was time to return to the office, Rick and Lance reluctantly got up and made their way outside.

Mrs Brookes was in the office when the pair got back. Standing by the desk with her eyes on the computer screen, she glanced across and quickly tapped a few keys to finish what she was doing. Then she straightened up and looked at Lance.

"There you are," she remarked. "You'd just gone out when I got here. The police called at the apartment this morning, and they've commandeered your laptop. They said they need it in relation to the accusations that have been made against the Petersons. They need it to rule out any of the conversations coming from it. I've bought you a replacement and thought I'd drop it here and explain what's happened. I'm about to go and visit someone, so I'll see you later."

Lance said nothing as he hung up his coat and crossed over to the window so that he could stare outside. Mrs Brookes watched him for a few moments before glancing at Rick; then looked back at Lance again. What could she do? No matter what she said, she got no response. She had no idea what was going through his mind.

"There is something that you can do," Rick said, keeping his eyes upon Lance. "Lance has been through so much since he arrived here. Thanks to Cindy, he's not been able to concentrate on work. He's not had the chance to learn nearly enough of what he has been expected to learn. It's only going to disappoint his father when he's expected to return. Maybe, if he's allowed to stay here for longer, he might feel more confident about returning. The biggest issue, though, is the Petersons. He really doesn't want to see them again. I think that Lance will be able to concentrate again after the Petersons have been dealt with. I don't think it's fair to expect too much of Lance at the moment. I only hope that his father will understand."

Mrs Brookes nodded slowly as she promised to talk to Blake again. She hesitated, as though intending to say more, but instead she turned and left the room. Rick watched her go; then moved over to where Lance was standing. Watching him carefully, Rick suggested that they sorted out his new laptop.

Eventually responding, Lance said that he only needed to get an internet connection, and he would do that when he got back to the apartment. Lance then realized as he looked around the room that his mother had disappeared. He didn't appear to be at all bothered about being deserted once more as he looked out of the window again. Mrs Brookes had said that she was going to visit someone, and who that person was was of no concern to him. Now he just wanted his mother to go home and leave him alone. Only then would he be able to relax and escape to some kind of fantasy world, where he could pretend that he was free to remain here for the rest of his life. There was one thing that he was certain of: he was going to make the most of whatever time he had here while he could.

Chapter 23

White clouds scudded across a bright blue sky as a blustery wind blew them on their way. The rain had stopped falling, and the ground was at last beginning to dry out. The dry weather had enticed many people out onto the hills; their cheeks and noses red, eyes watering and noses running.

Lance too was out there, though he had no intention of joining the other people who were marching along the hilltop. The climb up the hill quickly brought him to the trees that he was heading for, and reaching the wood, Lance barely glanced around him as he stepped between the trees. Suddenly intent upon reaching the lake, he made his way along the now familiar but unmarked path that wound its way through the trees. Only when he stepped out into the clearing did he hesitate; then head for the shores of the lake. The lake was, as always, bathed in that eerie white light, with mist shrouding the island at its centre.

Lance sat down on the pale green grass upon reaching his usual spot and gazed across at the island. Lost in his thoughts, he was unaware of anything that might be going on around him. Time always seemed to stand still here, and Lance was beginning to relax, with the time that had passed by the time someone stopped alongside him having no importance. Glancing around, he forced a nervous smile as he greeted Gwyn. He had not expected her to come, and certainly had not expected her to want to know him after what had happened. The only thing that he could do was to apologize for what his mother had done.

Gwyn sat down beside him and smiled. He was not to blame for anything that had happened. Lance could not bring himself to look at her. His mother should not have called in on her in the way that she had. She should not have tried to deal directly with Gwyn instead of her brother. His mother had been told, and Lance now believed that Gareth's refusal to carry on with any kind of deal had served her right. Gareth had every right to be livid with her.

"She flew back home yesterday, and did nothing but complain about how disappointed she was."

"Take no notice of Gareth," Gwyn urged. "He's the kind of person who sulks and bears a grudge for a while if he doesn't get his own way. He'll come round once he's had time to calm down. I'm flattered that your mother is so interested in what we do that she actually wants to sell our designs in America. It's rather exciting." Gwyn hesitated before telling him that she was glad that he had come here today and showed that he was still interested.

Lance gazed at her for a few long moments; then looked back at the island. In a way, it would have been much easier if she had been angry too. Instead, she was being much more than just a little understanding. Swallowing, he continued to stare across at the island.

"I hope that my mom's actions have not made your life difficult."

"I don't see Gareth much these days. He still lives in the flat over the shop. I only need to call him if there's anything that I need. He'll bring it over and act as though nothing has happened. It's just the way he is, and it really is best if you just ignore him like I do."

Gwyn's reply, despite having been half-expected, still surprised him. He remained unconvinced, though. It would be all too easy to predict what would happen if Gareth was to come here now and find them talking to each other. It did not take a genius to know that he would be anything but pleased.

Gwyn now also preferred to look across at the island. Its coastline was, as ever, constantly shifting and changing in the mists that were swirling around it. What Gareth thought did not concern her. He knew as much as they did that Lance's mother had acted alone. They all knew that Lance himself had not known anything about what his mother had planned to do. Gareth would never be able to justify blaming Lance.

"Your mother is concerned about you," Gwyn continued. "She knows that there is something on your mind. She wants to help you, but doesn't know how."

"It's nothing," Lance claimed, knowing that he would confide in her after hesitating for a moment. "My father is taking the Petersons to court. His lawyers have told him that every last detail needs to be revealed if they're going to do this properly. Everyone in the world except for me is going to know every last detail."

He had no choice but to let his father go ahead. If he did not, then he would never get the Petersons out of his life. Whether he liked it or not, there was no going back now. His own laptop would already have had everything that had ever been on it retrieved. As he had nothing to hide, that did not bother him at all. All they would find out about him would be his sudden interest in the local legend who had lived here many years ago. His father's lawyers were able to get the case heard quickly – at the beginning of August by all accounts. Lance was glad that he was here, well away from it all. The people in Boston were already discussing it, and Lance was glad that he could come here so that he could escape from it all.

Gwyn always listened to what he said without being judgemental in any way. Talking his problems through with her made it easier for him to get everything straight in his mind. He could then think more clearly and get a grip on the situation. If he did not have Avalon to come to and Gwyn to talk to, he knew what would have happened. He would have gone ahead and married Cindy without question. He would never have found the courage to confront his father so he could escape from her clutches, and whatever else it was that she had planned to do to him. It was all because of what Gwyn had said that he had found the courage that he needed. He could not thank her enough, but now his mother had repaid her by making her life difficult by trying to bypass Gareth and deal directly with Gwyn.

"She only did what she thought was best," Gwyn told him. "Her intentions were honourable enough. I'll see if I can talk Gareth round when he's calmed down. I can't see it being a problem, and it's nothing compared to what you're being forced to cope with at the moment."

Lance was not convinced. His mother had behaved in the same way that his father did. She had refused to listen, instead choosing to bulldoze on regardless of the consequences. All that she had succeeded in achieving was to give him one more thing to think about. She had aggravated the situation, and could so easily have cost him this friendship with Gwyn. Thankfully, he could still come here to Avalon and still had Gwyn's friendship. He could not afford to lose any of this. He could not afford to lose *her*. She was the only person he could really talk to, and without her friendship, he truly would be lost and very alone.

Lance stared across at the island, deep in thought. Then he suddenly drew breath and spoke without looking at Gwyn. When he had been confronted with the dagger the other day, he could only guess that it had been the second test. He had thought about it a lot over the last few days. Sensing Gwyn nodding, he asked if that dagger had in fact been Excalibur, the great king's sword. He had seen how the blade had lengthened while in the hand of the Lady of the Lake, and he had not been blind to the fact that it had been a full-sized sword by the time it disappeared beneath the water. He had sensed Morgan beginning her journey across the lake; her anger and frustration at his actions.

Gwyn smiled knowingly. His powers appeared to be growing with each test that he had passed. At the same time, Morgan's powers would be diminishing. She had now lost possession of both the Holy Grail and Excalibur, both of which had intensified the powers that she already possessed. That would make her more dangerous and more desperate to cling onto her advantage. The cup and sword would remain in the possession of the Lady of the Lake for now, and would remain so until Lance had undertaken the third and final test.

"Gwyn, they're all making a terrible mistake. I'm not the person they're seeking. I have no connection with this area."

"They don't make mistakes, Lance. I know that you've checked and checked again, and I can only assume that you *do* have a connection hidden away somewhere. Morgan would not waste her energy and risk losing the Holy Grail and Excalibur if you did not have the required connection."

Lance fell silent as he tried to work out what was going on. Gwyn sounded convinced, and was adamant that the shadows of the people who used to live there had not been mistaken.

"Do you know what the final test is?" he asked.

"Only Morgan knows the answer to that question," Gwyn told him, "and no-one has ever got past the first test before. What is happening now is new to all of us. We have no idea what the third and final test is, or how long it will be before you will be expected to face it. We only know that Morgan will make her move when she has the advantage."

With plenty to think about, Lance eventually got up and reluctantly headed away from the lake. The new revelations were at least taking his mind off his problems at home, and his mind was spinning as he drove back to his apartment. He waited until he was stepping out of the lift before hunting through his pockets for his door key, stopping sharply upon noticing a familiar and unwelcome figure standing by his door. Cindy was waiting for him, watching him intently.

Lance's voice was cold as he asked her what she was doing here. His mind raced as he pushed his key into the lock, jumping and looking round at Cindy when she reached out and took hold of his hand. Pulling free from her grasp, Lance unlocked his door and pushed it open.

"Please, Lance. I only want to talk; let you know that I've made a huge mistake," Cindy told him. "Won't you forgive me and give me another chance?"

Lance stepped into the apartment, turning back so that he could pull his key out of the lock and shut the door. This brought him face to face with Cindy again, and Lance noted the desperation in her eyes. She was not interested in him. She was only interested in saving her own skin. There could be only one reason why she should want him to take her back. A sudden confidence engulfed Lance as he stared at her, giving him the courage to stand up to her.

"Go home, Cindy. You've wasted your time, coming here. I never want to see you again. And as for your claims about your baby, I've worked out the dates, and they don't add up. I was already over here."

"I must have got them wrong. Lance, I've realized over these past few weeks that I can't live without you. I only want to sit down and talk things through. I'd never do anything to hurt you. I couldn't possibly do any of those things to you. Phil was the one who wanted to do that."

"There's nothing to talk about," Lance abruptly interrupted her, "and I have no idea what you'd planned to do. I haven't seen any of the evidence. My parents have, though, and it's incited my father to take action against you. He knows that I only want you to leave me alone. Anything else is what my father wants. I want nothing more to do with you."

Lance firmly shut his door and leaned back against it. Closing his eyes for a few moments, he heard Cindy shouting to him through the door. She was clearly in no hurry to move away. In a bid to shut out the sound of her voice, Lance moved into the living room and closed that door behind him as well. Then he moved across to the window and stared out at the millions of lights that were shining out into the darkness. It was proving impossible to shut out Cindy's voice, but still Lance tried desperately to ignore her. All that he could do was hope and pray that she would go away and leave him alone. She could say whatever she liked. He was not going to give her the second chance that she wanted.

Chapter 24

"Why didn't you call me?" Rick asked.

Lance continued to stare at the desk before him. Rick had wanted to know what was troubling him, and now he was reacting exactly as Lance had expected him to. Lance had seen the police arrive yesterday evening after one of his neighbours had complained about the noise that Cindy was making. One of them had rung his bell, and had joined him when he had nervously dared to answer his door.

"There was no need," Lance told him, his voice quiet. "It's all been dealt with. I have to learn how to deal with this kind of thing sometime. I can't expect others to keep on bailing me out, even though I wasn't the one who called the police yesterday. I'm sure she'd have given up eventually even if they hadn't arrived."

"You should still have let me know." Rick sounded annoyed. "You must call me if it happens again. Have you told your parents?"

Rick watched Lance carefully. He did not react at all for a few moments, and then he checked the time on his watch. No, he had not told his parents yet, and was not going to until it was a more respectable time in Boston. There was plenty of time for him to make that call, considering that Cindy had been cautioned by the police. If she did not stay away from him, he could have her immediately deported back to America.

Then Lance suggested that they should be working, but Rick was determined not to give in easily. There was still so much that Lance had not told him, and he was going to find everything out before accepting that the subject no longer needed to be discussed.

"Why did she come over here to see you?" he asked.

"She wants me to forgive her and give her another chance." Lance refused to look at Rick as he spoke. "She says that she's made a big mistake, and that I really am the father of her baby. She claims that she must have got the dates wrong. No, she didn't fool me this time. Rick, I did a lot of thinking last night, and I want to see the evidence that you got against her. I want to see it all so I can see what she's said and done. I'm scared that she will fool me if I don't know what she's planning. And this is the only way I can think of to make sure that she'll never be able to talk me round."

Rick was far from happy with Lance's request. He could not let Lance see what Cindy had planned to do to him. It was something that no-one should have to see; something that should be kept locked away and hidden for all time. Lance, however, was just as determined to see what Rick had gathered. It was all going to become very public when it went to court anyway; surely it would be better for him to know beforehand? Lance believed that he had a right to know, and besides, how would it look if she succeeded in talking him round purely because he didn't know what it was that she had planned to do? Rick knew how convincing she could be. He needed to see the evidence.

Rick remained silent as he gazed at Lance. He could hardly argue with what Lance had just said. Lance had sounded logical, and had made perfect sense. Yet Rick still could not help but doubt that this was the right thing to do. No matter how reluctant he was, however, Lance was determined to see every last detail, no matter how small and insignificant it might seem. Hesitating, Rick sighed as he slowly gave in. Before he fetched the evidence, though, he wanted another key cutting for Lance's front door. Rick wanted to be able to get in without force if needed.

Lance eyed him suspiciously for a few long moments, Rick staring defiantly back at him. Then Lance got up off his chair and pulled a key out of his coat pocket. Rick was quick to take it; his eyes still upon Lance as he moved across to the office door and sent Will out to get another key cut. It was clear that Rick was anything but happy about showing Lance the evidence. If that was what Lance really wanted, though, then he would reluctantly go and fetch the DVD and memory stick.

Lance remained determined to see for himself the evidence that Rick had gathered. Surely Rick knew that he would react in exactly the same way if he were in Lance's position? Realizing that he had no other choice, Rick made his way down to the company's vaults that were in the basement of the building. There he collected two small and insignificant-looking envelopes before returning to the office. Lance was standing by the window and staring outside, Rick still insisting that they waited until Will had returned. With two identical keys in his hand, Rick handed the original back to Lance.

Rick and Lance pushed the keys into their trouser pockets; then Rick checked one last time that Lance really did want to see this evidence for himself. Still extremely reluctant, he loaded the DVD into the computer and moved to stand behind Lance's chair. There was no going back now. Rick said nothing as he desperately tried to keep his eyes upon Lance instead of being distracted by what was on the computer.

With his eyes glued to the screen, Lance watched in silence. He recognized the apartment immediately, and knew exactly where this film had been made. Now he could understand why he had been accused of making it. There was nothing that he could say as Cindy willingly confessed to everything while making her move on this unknown man. There could be no denying that this person was Cindy, or what her intentions were.

Lance continued to stare at the blank screen after the DVD had come to an end. How could she have called him all of those things? He had only ever done whatever she had demanded, just to please her. Everything that he had ever done had been for her benefit. Feeling a hand on his shoulder, Lance looked round and gradually returned to reality as he focused upon Rick. Then he swallowed, looked away and stared back into space again. Rick squeezed his shoulder as he apologized and suggested that he tried to forget about it. Cindy had revealed the kind of person that she really was. She was heartless, and clearly had no idea of the thoroughly decent man that he was. Cindy did not deserve him at all.

Lance still refused to look at him. He wanted to see the internet conversation now. Rick eyed him dubiously, Lance quickly cutting in and insisting that he wanted to see it. He wanted to see it all. He needed to know what everyone else on the planet was about to discover. Still, Rick was uncomfortable about showing him. This was what they had been trying to stop his father from revealing. Mr Brookes was determined to reveal all though, and Rick knew that there was nothing else that he could do. Sliding the DVD back into its envelope, Rick moved back and watched

Lance load the information from the memory stick onto the computer.

With his eyes fixed upon the screen, Lance began to read every last word of the conversation. So this was what Cindy had been doing on her laptop, and right in front of him too. This was why she had quickly hidden it every time he came near. Everything that Cindy and Phil had said was sickening. This was why his parents and Rick had not wanted him to see it. This was why his mother and Rick had not wanted his father to use it in court. This was why Cindy had wanted him to take her back. She really was only trying to save her own skin. This was why she had come all the way over here to see him: she was trying to stop his father from bringing a court case against her and her parents.

Lance sat motionless for a few minutes when he had read to the end of the conversation. Rick was apologizing again, Lance vaguely aware of him as he asked him if he was all right. Slowly he nodded, but Rick knew that, in reality, he was far from all right. Lance was feeling too numb to feel anything at the moment. Rick could only guess what was going through his mind as he cleared the entire conversation from the computer. He did not want Lance to be able to read every last and sickening detail again. He did not want Lance to look at what Cindy had really had in store for him. Lance could only stare into space, every word that he had just read revolving around and around in his head.

Rick slid the memory stick back into its envelope. Anxious to get them safely returned to the vault, he was acutely aware that Lance was in no state to go anywhere. He did not want to leave him on his own either, though. Rick could not tell what was going through Lance's mind, and so how the evidence had affected him, Rick did not know. Not knowing what to do, Rick decided to take a chance. Warning Lance against going anywhere while he returned the envelopes to the vault, Rick was gone. Lance looked distant, as though unable to take anything in.

Returning the two envelopes seemed to take a frustratingly long time, and Rick was fretting over having left Lance alone as he securely locked the envelopes away. He was glad to leave the basement after waiting impatiently for the lift, and back in the office, he spent the next couple of agonizing minutes answering the staff's questions. At last he could make his way across to the smaller office and open the door, stopping abruptly and going cold as he stared at the empty chair.

"Where's Lance?" he asked.

"Oh, he's gone to fetch some coffee from the canteen," one of the others said.

Rick did not like the answer. Lance's coat was still hanging where he had left it, yet still Rick felt insecure as he made his way down to the canteen. He was losing precious time as he searched the building for Lance, eventually seeking out Graham.

"He told me that you wanted him to fetch some software from across town," the chauffeur said.

Rick went cold again, his heart pounding as his mind raced. He knew exactly where Lance would be heading. There was no software to collect. There were no doubts in Rick's mind where Lance was going, and this time he did not know whether he would be able to reach Avalon in time.

Chapter 25

Lance gave no thought to locking the car when he parked at the side of the road and hurried up the nearby hillside. He could only focus upon getting to Avalon. He walked quickly, occasionally reaching down with his hand as though steadying himself as he climbed the hill. There was the brightest of blue skies overhead, white clouds scattered across its wide expanse while birds scudded about before hovering on the thermals that were rising above the hills. None of that mattered, though. Lance was focusing entirely upon one thing.

Very few people were about, save for the occasional hardy rambler intent upon reaching their destination as they strode across the hilltop. Lance saw none of them. He was aware of nothing, not even the fact that he had left his coat behind in the office. He was didn't feel the icy air, and was not huddling or shivering in his shirt and jacket as he hurried on up the hill. The wood was drawing ever closer, Lance at last stepping in among the trees. On he went, not noticing how the wind had stopped blowing and the temperature had risen by the time he reached the shores of the lake.

The white light was, as always, steadily shining as the mist swirled and shifted over the surface of the water that surrounded the island. Lance slowly made his way around the shoreline, staring across at Avalon and stopping only when he kicked something with his foot. Looking down, he stared at the plain wooden chalice that was lying on the grass in front of his feet. Lance reached down; then suddenly pulled back as he continued to gaze down at it. The Holy Grail – but what was it doing here? It was supposed to be safely in the hands of the Lady of the Lake.

Lance looked up quickly when he heared a voice, and stared in awe and admiration at the large man who was standing in the boat that was drifting nearby on the water. Clad in armour, his eyes were steely yet kind as he smiled encouragingly at him. He had sensed that Lance had come here to see him and seek counsel. He had been expecting him, and was ready to give him the advice that he sought.

It was time for Lance to escape from the torment and pain that he so needlessly suffered. He only needed to pick up the chalice that was lying at his feet and then join him on this boat. The water was shallow here; all that he needed to do was wade across and climb into the boat. The man could then take him to his sanctuary and shield him from everything that plagued him beyond these woods.

Lance swallowed as he continued to stare at him. He had never expected to meet this legendary hero. Not even in his wildest dreams did he ever think that he would come face to face with the mighty King Arthur, and yet now that this great man was here before him, Lance had expected the king to utter only words of wisdom. He had been seeking the mighty king's counsel; his guidance on how best to deal with what was happening to him, yet he was being encouraged to pick up the chalice and wade out to the boat that was drifting nearby.

Lance reached down and picked up the chalice; then he took a couple of slow and tentative steps forwards before stopping by the water's edge. Again he stared at this mightiest of men before him. King Arthur was offering him the opportunity to join him on Avalon, where he would be able to shelter until this storm had passed. The boat was right here before him as it drifted sedately nearby. All that he had to do was make his way across to it through the shallow water while he still had the chance.

Lance suddenly stepped back and shook his head. Throwing the cup across the lake, he turned away as it travelled through the air before immediately sinking as it hit the water. Oblivious to anything that was happening behind him, Lance hurried away from the lake. Voices were calling out to him as they desperately tried to talk to him. Lance ignored them all, shutting them out and almost breaking into a run as he broke free from the trees and headed back down the open hillside towards the car.

Rick hurried back up to the office and snatched up his car keys. More precious minutes were being lost. Why had he not realized that Lance would do something like this? Catching sight of Lance's coat, Rick snatched it and then ran back out of the office again. He took the stairs, feeling that it would be quicker than waiting for the lift to take him to the ground floor. He raced down as quickly as he could; then hurried out of the back of the building to the underground car park.

Rick fumbled as he pushed the key into the lock of his car before dragging the door open and throwing the two coats onto the passenger seat. Frustration was quickly rising as he struggled to push the key into the ignition. This sense of urgency was making him rush too much, and make stupid mistakes. Lance had a good twenty minutes' lead on him, easily enough time to ensure that Rick would already be too late. As he headed out of the car park, he could only hope and pray that the traffic would be light today.

Rick was out of luck. The amount of traffic on the streets of Bristol was much heavier than usual, Rick cursing constantly as he battled on. By the time he had succeeded in breaking free from the city streets so that he could drive along the open road, Lance's advantage had risen to half an hour. There did not appear to be much hope of saving him now, though that was not going to stop Rick from at least trying. Lance might have convinced Graham that he had wanted the car to run a simple errand, but Rick was not going to be fooled for a moment. Lance would be heading to Avalon, and could well be there already.

Rick cursed the length of time that it was taking him to reach the hills as he moved more quickly across the valley. He drove on, vaguely aware of breaking the speed limit in his haste. At last he approached the bottom of a familiar hillside, staring in disbelief at the narrow grass verge that ran alongside the road. There was no car to be seen. There was nothing.

Rick pulled over and hesitated for a few moments before quickly making up his mind. He knew that he had to go and check the lake while he was here. Lance may, after all, have parked elsewhere in a bid to throw him off his trail. Rick knew that he would never forgive himself if he later discovered that he had thrown away this only chance to save him.

Grabbing the two coats, Rick climbed out of his car and pulled on his coat as he hurried up the hillside. He had to get to the lake, and he had to get there in time. He should have kept Lance with him; he should have refused to let him see those internet conversations with Cindy Peterson's derisory comments. The film had been bad enough, and he should have insisted that they stopped at that.

Rick did not stop when he reached the wood. He ran on through the trees until he reached the lake in the clearing, and from there he made his way around the shoreline, stopping only when he reached the spot where Lance usually stood. The place was deserted, the lake tranquil and still. Rick stared about him, at a loss as to what he should do next. Hesitating, he turned and walked back out of the wood, and once out on the open hillside, he pulled his mobile phone out of his coat pocket and called the office. There was, however, still no sign of Lance there.

Rick returned to his car. Where else could Lance have got to? Sighing with overwhelming frustration, he walked around the front of his car towards the driver's door, staring down at the ground and suddenly stopping as he caught his breath. Another car had been here, and recently, judging by the fresh tracks. Rick's heart was beating faster. Lance had indeed come here. Where had he run to when he had left, though? Rick's mind was racing. He could think of nowhere. He had expected to find him here at Avalon. He had found the place deserted, and now he had no idea where Lance might hide.

Rick reached into his pocket for his car keys. Pulling them out, he slowly focused on the spare key to Lance's apartment. Could it be possible that Lance had gone home? Rick pondered that possibility for a moment or two; then he wrenched open his car door and climbed in. He could think of nowhere else that Lance might well have gone.

Rick cursed the traffic yet again before eventually pulling up outside the apartment block. The company car was here, Rick quickly checking it over before looking up at the building and hurrying inside. Pushing the spare key into the lock, he let himself in and called out Lance's name as he looked up and down the hallway. The kitchen and living room checked, Rick moved along the hallway and pushed the bedroom door open. Lance was in the room, hastily forcing his clothes into a bag.

"Lance?" Rick broke the silence as Lance glanced round at him. "What are you doing?"

"I'm going home," Lance stated, continuing to push his clothes into his bag.

"Why?" Rick moved further into the room when he got no answer. Again he asked why as he stopped alongside Lance.

Lance refused to look at him as he told him that he did not want to stay here any longer. He wanted to return home to Boston. He wanted to get away from here and never come back. He was still packing, stopping only when Rick took hold of his arm. Rick wanted to sit down with a coffee, so that they could talk this through. Lance reluctantly gave in, despite his mind already being made up. And no amount of talking was going to change it.

Rick made some coffee; then sat down with Lance in the living room. He could only assume that it was the evidence that Lance had seen that had made up his mind, and Lance was telling him nothing that should make him think otherwise. It was not going to be that simple, though. Rick was looking after Lance's passport to prevent him from returning home before it was deemed safe for him to do so. He was going to have to call his parents before he could hand it over, and tell them what had happened before any decision could be made.

Lance stared at him; then seemed to give in. He was not going to stop Rick calling his father. There would be no point in trying to argue with him. Instead, he crossed over to the window and stared outside while Rick made the call.

"I'm sorry, Lance." Rick pushed his mobile phone back into his pocket. "Your parents have decided to fly over and discuss this before they decide whether it's safe for you to return home just yet."

Lance said nothing. That was the answer that he had been expecting, and waiting for a couple more days would not make any difference. Rick forced a smile as he apologized. There was nothing else that he could do. Now they could only wait.

Chapter 26

Rick's hand hovered just in front of the doorbell as he hesitated for a moment or two before daring to ring it. Dressed in jeans, sweatshirt and coat, Gwyn looked completely different as she stood beside him. The expression on her face was enough to show how nervous she was feeling. Long moments passed, and then they heard someone inside the apartment moving towards the door as Gwyn looked up and down the corridor. The door opened slightly as Mrs Brookes peered out and recognized them before opening it further.

Rick greeted her politely. Gwyn, he explained, had called in at the office. He now believed that something had happened at Avalon that could be the real reason behind Lance deciding that he wanted to return home. Mrs Brookes nodded as she invited the pair inside, quickly closing the door behind them once they had stepped through.

The revelation explained why Lance was adamantly refusing to go to the lake. She had been unable to understand why he had suddenly been so determined to return home. There had been no explanation for this sudden change of heart, and Lance had simply insisted over and over again that he did not want to remain here for a moment longer. His father, though, still believed that he should remain here. It was not safe for him to return home just yet.

Gwyn hung back out of sight as they approached the living room doorway. She was wary of what Lance's reaction would be, making her nervous about revealing her presence. What he was likely to say, she had no idea. Instead she hovered near the doorway so that she could hear what was being said as Rick and Mrs Brookes disappeared into the room without realizing that she was no longer following them. She slowly moved forwards, stopping in the doorway and refusing to move any further.

Blake Brookes was standing by the window. With his hands behind his back, his bulky frame was silhouetted by the daylight that streamed into the room through the window behind him. It gave him the advantage, as Rick now had the sun in his eyes when he addressed him. Lance sat on the settee and said nothing as Rick informed them of Cindy's actions when she was last at Lance's apartment. She was staying at a local hotel, and appeared to be in no hurry to return to America. She had been to a private detective agency, and had paid them to dig up what dirt they could on Lance and his father. What her next move was to be, Rick did not yet know.

"Who are you?" Blake Brookes suddenly caught sight of Gwyn standing in the doorway. His demand made her swallow as she stepped back a little, as though ready to flee. The question made Lance quickly look round at her.

"Gwyn has come to see Lance," Rick explained. "She's hoping that he will agree to return to Avalon with her."

"No." Lance's response was instant and decisive. "Nothing is going to make me go back there. I never want to see the place or any of them again."

"You can at least listen to what she wants to tell you." Rick sounded a little annoyed.

"I don't want to hear anything," Lance insisted. "I'm not going back there. It'll be a waste of time."

"Lance —"

"I'm not going back there, Rick, and I'm not going to play any more of their silly games. I'm not interested in any of it anymore."

Gwyn gazed sadly at him; then turned and fled. Rick took a step after her, before stopping and staring back at Lance. He was disappointed and ashamed of him. After all of the unconditional support that Gwyn had given him during his time here, the very least that he could have done was to listen to what she had to say. She had certainly not deserved to be spoken to in such a way. If this was how he intended to treat people, Rick did not want to know him any longer. Hesitating for the briefest of moments, Rick turned and hurried out of the apartment.

Gwyn had hurried down the stairs and emerged from the building before Rick managed to catch up with her. She could see the genuineness in his eyes as he apologized to her. Rick had not envisaged the reaction that they had just had from Lance. It appeared to be out of character, as though he was quickly turning into a younger version of his father, and Rick could see no harm in Lance returning to Avalon one more time.

Lance had crossed over to the window and was now staring down at Rick and Gwyn. How dare Rick suggest that he had not met King Arthur the other day? He had not been there. He had not seen what he had seen or heard the words that he had heard. He had not watched as the wooden chalice sunk into the waters of the lake. Rick knew nothing.

Gwyn appeared to be reluctantly climbing into Rick's car. He was undoubtedly going to give her a lift home, back to a time gone by when others had walked upon this earth. Lance remained silent as the car disappeared out of sight. They were gone, and out of his life. Lance continued to stare at the empty street. It was over. He had broken free from those ghosts from the past.

Lance suddenly went cold as he caught his breath. What had he done? It was too late to stop

Rick now. With his blood running cold, Lance turned away from the window and grabbed his trainers. He needed to go to Avalon, before something truly awful happened. He had been wrong, and now he could only hope that he could get to Avalon in time so that he could put things right.

Rick watched Gwyn head away up the hillside; then sighed as he started the engine of his car. The company car was pulling up behind him, Rick watching it in his mirror before switching the engine off again and climbing back out of his car. The back door of the car was already open, Lance glancing at Rick as he climbed out before looking up the hill. Gwyn was already close to the trees, and Lance ignored Rick as he scrambled up the hillside after her.

Gwyn was unaware of his presence as she made her way to the lake. Arthur and Guinevere were waiting patiently for her, both watching her approach as they stood upon the pale grass. Her sadness was clear to see, her eyes betraying her as she apologized. She had failed, and had not even been given the chance to explain. Lance had not been interested. He had not wanted to know what had happened. She had been given no opportunity to speak. Instead, he had simply told her that he was never going to return here.

Guinevere smiled kindly as she moved across to where Gwyn was standing. Gwyn needed more faith. She needed to believe in herself more. They could understand why he had reacted in this way. Guinevere did not believe that she had failed. Gwyn gazed across the lake to the island. She was not convinced. Guinevere slid a comforting arm around her, and they stood in silence, gazing over the water to Avalon. Then, slowly, they appeared to merge and become one, Gwyn's modern clothing dissolving into Guinevere's white robe.

"No!" Lance called out his objection as he burst out of the trees, before coming to an abrupt stop. Now he could only stare at the scene that was before him. Guinevere was the one Lance could see as she looked round at him, and Lance gazed at her and hesitated before speaking.

"Please, don't go," he said. "I'm sorry about what I said. I was wrong for not wanting to listen to you. It was Morgan who I saw the other day, wasn't it? I should have realized that she had set another test. Please don't leave. Please don't tell me that I'm already too late."

Gwyn looked at him for a few long moments before turning away again. She was not about to leave this world. She was simply being comforted by Guinevere, and was now being advised to say nothing just yet.

Arthur was moving forwards, Lance turning slightly to look at him. Gazing up at him, he swallowed. Somehow, he could sense that the genuine King Arthur was now standing before him. By all accounts, Lance should have felt intimidated by the giant who was towering high above him. The king's eyes, however, were soft and kind, making Lance feel humbled and yet welcomed here. He was feeling ashamed, too, for having mistaken Morgan for him. Now he was looking at the very real prospect of losing the one person who had supported him unconditionally through his darkest days, and he was prepared to do anything to ensure that she stayed.

"Would you be prepared to accept this from me?" Arthur gazed down at him as he held up a simple chain.

Lance hesitated for a moment as he baulked at the possible consequences. The chain was held up in front of him, and Lance looked across to where Gwyn and Guinevere were standing. He could only gaze at Gwyn, the only thought that was running through his mind being his confession that he would do anything to save her. Lance swallowed as he looked back up at Arthur, and then he bowed his head. He had said that he would do anything to prevent Gwyn leaving, and he had this chance to prove that he would do just that.

Lance kept his eyes upon the pair of large, armour-clad feet that were before him as he felt the chain being slipped over his head and hung around his neck. Armour-covered hands were then placed upon his shoulders, Lance looking back up at the man standing before him. Arthur smiled down at him as he thanked him for freeing him so that he could now return from Avalon. The white light shone more brightly, blinding Lance for a few moments as a strong breeze swirled around him. He could sense it driving deep inside him, until the light faded once more so that the greens of the trees and the grass came back into focus.

Lance could see nothing as he stared ahead of him. Arthur had deserted him once more, and everything else became more distant. It all felt unreal. The white light was fading once more as the darkness increased. He had made the wrong choice, and Guinevere's reassuring words did nothing to allay his fears. The darkness was enveloping him, and Lance was unable to do anything to stop it as his senses slipped away and finally deserted him.

Chapter 27

Lance slowly began to stir, unaware that his mother and Rick had somehow succeeded in stopping his father from charging forwards and demanding to know what was going on. He eventually opened his eyes and stared up at the person who was beside him, before tentatively sitting up. He was feeling lightheaded, and completely detached from his surroundings.

"What's going on?" he asked, still looking and feeling dazed.

"You've just met King Arthur," Gwyn reminded him, her voice calm and quiet.

Lance gazed at her as his memories flooded back. Looking down, he took hold of the simple chain that hung around his neck. King Arthur had given it to him before the light had blinded him, and a blank darkness had then engulfed him. He was still here, and was still alive. More important, though, was that they had not taken Gwyn with them when they had retreated to Avalon. She was still here, and now that he was looking at her again, he could see that she was not wearing one of her dresses.

"Arthur asked me to look for you." Gwyn smiled. "And I didn't think that the people of Bristol would be too keen if I didn't dress normally."

Gwyn took a small bottle of water out of her coat pocket and offered it to him. With his eyes fixed firmly upon her, Lance tentatively took the bottle. Her soft, light brown hair was reflecting the white light that illuminated the lake. Tied back and tucked away inside her coat, he could not see how long it was. She looked so different, dressed like this. He did not want to take his eyes off her, and he wanted to savour every moment. Then he opened the bottle and looked away from her as he drank the water.

Blake Brookes had been about to stride forwards when his wife and Rick stopped him. He was indignant and irritated; and stared at them in disbelief. Had they not seen what had just happened? They must have seen what he had just seen – that man, the one who had been clad in medieval armour, had towered over his son, and would have towered over Blake himself if he had been standing in Lance's place. As the light brightened, he had melted away in front of his very eyes into a cloud of swirling smoke that twisted and circled around Lance before quickly disappearing. The light had then faded, as Lance looked about him as though in a daze before sinking to the ground.

Nancy Brookes had stopped her husband from rushing out from the trees. Instead, she urged him to watch and listen while remaining out of sight. She had been here before, and had already witnessed things that simply could not be explained. If they kept back and listened, they would learn so much more. Lance would talk to Gwyn in a way that he did not talk to anyone else, and she would be able to find out what was going through his mind. Staring at his wife, Blake then looked back at the pair, who were still beside the shores of the lake. What was Nancy thinking? Blake had never stood back and listened in his life. Yet somehow, that was exactly what he was now doing.

"What happened when you were last here?" Gwyn asked, taking the bottle from Lance.

Lance stared at her for a few moments; then turned and gazed across the water to the island. "Cindy turned up. She wanted me to give her another chance. I told Rick that I wanted to see the evidence against her so that she had no chance of me forgiving her. I didn't expect to see or hear what I did, though, and I did what I've always done and fled here at the first opportunity, like the coward I am. The chalice was here on the grass when I got here, and then King Arthur appeared. He wanted me to join him on Avalon. He told me I only needed to wade across to the boat he was in."

Lance could sense Gwyn's eyes upon him as she watched him carefully. He had fallen silent, and continued to gaze ahead of him. Gwyn was urging him to continue, and Lance kept his eyes upon the mist-shrouded island as he gathered his thoughts.

"I was really disappointed. I mean, how could such a great and noble warrior suggest that I just gave up and joined him? I had expected so much more from him. I was feeling disillusioned and cheated out of everything that I had believed in; so I just picked up the chalice, threw it into the lake and walked away. I thought I'd get the inspiration that I needed to carry on if I came here, and in meeting King Arthur himself, I'd expected great words of wisdom to help me battle on. But I didn't get them, so I went home and started to pack so I could go home and not come back. Then Rick turned up and reminded me that he's got my passport."

Lance looked at Gwyn again. He had felt trapped, and had not known what to do. He knew that Rick would try to talk him out of leaving, just like he had known that his parents would fly back over here and tell him that it was still not safe for him to go back to Boston. They had wanted him to remain here, and had believed that it had been the evidence that he had seen that had made him want to return to America. He had said nothing about having come here, and had let them believe what they wanted to believe.

He had wanted to forget about what had happened here.

"The chalice that you threw into the lake was not the Holy Grail," Gwyn told him. "It was a replica that Morgan used to try to fool you. By doing what you did – throwing it into the lake after rejecting her offer – you have successfully trapped Morgan so that she can no longer do any harm. She must have sensed that you were vulnerable and more likely to be fooled by her deceit, but you've proven to be much stronger than she realized. But what about your other problem – the one that brought you here on that day?"

"Cindy? What about her? My father is sorting all of that out. I don't need to think about her. My father is not a coward like I am. He doesn't run away from things like I do. My father has every right to be disappointed in me. He is strong and capable, and knows exactly what to do."

Gwyn quietly insisted that Lance was no coward. There were so many other ways for him to demonstrate how brave he was. He had, in fact, already done it. He had already stood up to Gareth and his own father, and he had even stood up to the person whom he had believed to be King Arthur. It was all too easy for anyone to be completely awestruck by the great man; to believe that every course of action he suggested was the right one to take. After all, how could they not be, with all of the noble and heroic deeds that he had once performed? How could he possibly be wrong? Yet Lance had had the courage to stand up to him, and even tell him that he was wrong.

Lance stared into space as he tried to take in what Gwyn had told him. He was no coward. He had a great deal of courage. If he had been a coward, he would have fallen at the first hurdle. He would have accepted the chalice when Morgan had first offered it to him. His courage had proved to be even greater than the courage that King Arthur himself had possessed. Lance's courage was a quiet courage, a courage that was not always seen and was rarely acknowledged. He had shown that courage when he had returned here today and faced the person whom he had believed that he had met the other day. He was held in the highest esteem here. He was revered and respected, and he had just freed Arthur from Avalon. He had at last enabled him to return to this world.

Lance swallowed as he looked away in an attempt to hide his disappointment. King Arthur had returned, and he would undoubtedly want to claim Gwyn for his own. Unable to look her in the eye, he sounded less than enthusiastic as he offered to help her look for him. Gwyn smiled wistfully. She already knew who he was. She knew whose form he had assumed. She even knew exactly where he was right now.

Lance stared at the ground in front of his feet. There had to be something that he could do for her. She had done so much for him, yet she had taken nothing for herself.

"You believed in Arthur and Avalon," Gwyn told him, "and that means so much more to me than you could possibly realize. You should be resting and rebuilding your strength after everything that has happened here."

Lance watched her stand up, before getting to his feet himself. At last he noticed the three people who were standing in the nearby trees. He appeared genuinely surprised to see them, but his father was oblivious to his surprise as he broke the silence. It was time that they went back home.

Mr Brookes was taken by surprise himself when Lance dared to resist him as he began to guide him away. Returning to where Gwyn was still standing, Lance wanted to know if he would be able to see her again. He wanted to take her out to dinner somewhere, so he could thank her properly for everything that she had done for him. Gwyn smiled kindly as she accepted his offer, and told him that he knew she would always be here if he needed to see her.

Lance smiled nervously, and then hesitated before turning and crossing back to where his parents and Rick were waiting for him. Gwyn was still standing by the shores of the lake when he glanced back at her once more, and then his father was guiding him away and back to Rick's car. It was time, Mr Brookes decided, to stop this nonsense. He ordered Rick to leave Lance and his mother at the apartment before taking him to the office. He undoubtedly had a lot of work to catch up on.

Lance was sitting on the settee when his mother handed him a mug of coffee. He looked up at her, and then away again as he apologized for being a nuisance and dragging them back to England.

Mrs Brookes sat down beside him. They had been concerned about him. They had not been able to anticipate how much the evidence against the Petersons would shock him.

"That didn't shock me, Mom," Lance told her. "It was King Arthur, or at least the person I thought was King Arthur. I felt totally let down by the suggestion he made. I'm not the least bit bothered about the Petersons – I know that they'll never be able to do what they'd planned to do. I know that my father will easily deal with them."

"Oh, Lance! Your father is not as indestructible as you think, and he's nothing like as brave as you believe. He has an army of lawyers who do all the fighting for him. He simply pays them and then stands back and takes all the glory for himself. He's anything but courageous."

"He's still prepared to put his reputation on the line for me. It could easily go horribly wrong. He could still lose everything."

Mrs Brookes smiled. That was not going to happen. As powerful as the Petersons were, even they could not hope to win against the evidence that they had against them. Their only real option was to agree to an out-of-court settlement. Lance had nothing to fear. None of them had anything to fear. There was nothing that could possibly go wrong.

Chapter 28

It was early February, and the ground was waterlogged with the incessant rain that had fallen throughout the winter. Grey clouds hung ominously in the sky, while a squally wind blew the light rain that was falling. Wearing a coat to protect himself against this inclement weather, Lance squinted every time that he looked up to ensure that he was climbing the hill in the right direction, until he eventually reached the welcome sanctuary of the wood.

Three weeks had passed since he had met the genuine King Arthur at Avalon. He was feeling different after that experience, and somehow appeared to have gained a lot of confidence in his own abilities. No-one could explain the sudden change in him; not even Lance himself. It had first been revealed when he had calmly and abruptly sent the visiting Cindy on her way before his father could intervene, and ever since he had continued to surprise and impress both his mother and his exacting father. Then, a week after Cindy had flown back to Boston, they too had boarded an aeroplane and returned home. Lance had wanted to be certain that they really *had* boarded that plane, and so he had driven them to the airport and watched them go.

Then he had driven straight over to Avalon and sat by the shores of the lake until Gwyn had joined him. Only then had he revealed his insecurity. Suddenly he doubted whether King Arthur would actually agree to let him take her out for dinner in order to thank her for everything that she had done for him. Gwyn, however, had smiled kindly, and had been ready for him when he picked her up later that day.

Lance paused for a few moments after stepping into the shelter of the trees. What excuse could he possibly give for wanting to see Gwyn today? The only reason for being here at all was an overwhelming desire to come to Avalon. That at least was true – the desire to come here was simply too strong to resist. There was no excuse to give. He had needed to come here today; yet some unknown and unseen force had compelled him to make this journey. The reality was that there was nothing in this world that could have stopped him.

Lance moved on, that invisible force drawing him through the trees to the lake. It was still here, the water still tranquil and serene; its black depths, as always, covered by that ever-shifting layer of mist. He had had plenty of time to think over the last three weeks, and it had not taken him long to realize that if he had believed and accepted Morgan's deceit, he would have drowned in these waters. They were undeniably treacherous, and he would have been dragged under immediately and held there until all life had drained out of him. There would have been no reaching Avalon to be by King Arthur's side. Instead, an unimaginable hell would have been waiting for him as he failed the third and final test.

Lance kept his eyes upon the island as he made his way around the shores of the lake. Then, upon reaching that very familiar spot, he hesitated before sitting down. With the grass glowing beneath the white light that shone constantly, the air felt warm and dry, in sharp contrast to the weather that was beyond the borders of the wood. Everything had remained constant, the calm atmosphere enabling him to think more rationally. Time really did not seem to matter here.

It was possible to sit quietly for hours here, the amount of time that had actually passed only being realized when Lance stepped back out into the harsh reality of the world that was beyond these borders. It was as though time had stood still here at the very moment King Arthur had been carried away to Avalon. Lance could only wonder how he could have been so determined to turn his back and leave all of this behind. Yet Gwyn had told him that Arthur had finally been released from his prison, free to return to this world. That he could not deny. He had actually been here when it had happened; he had met the great man himself, and had been in awe of him while in his presence. Reaching up, Lance took hold of the chain that King Arthur himself had placed around his neck, and glanced round as Gwyn sat down beside him. Then he looked again, just to be sure that she *had* joined him, as he had hoped that she would. He could not stop himself from smiling, his eyes meeting hers as he greeted her. She was wearing jeans, a jumper and a short, waterproof jacket, and her trainers were already beginning to look well worn.

"Hi. You're wearing modern clothes again," he greeted her, pausing as he quickly looked at the ground in front of his feet. " I hope King Arthur will forgive me for saying this, but you looked stunning the other night. I guess he came here with you today?"

"He was already here when I arrived," Gwyn told him.

Lance quickly looked at her; then carefully looked about them. Everything was still and silent, and he could see no other sign of life. Long moments passed, and then he looked back down at the ground.

"I hope he doesn't mind me coming here so I can see you."

"Lance, King Arthur has returned to this world, but not in the guise that we all know and recognize." Gwyn spoke quietly and calmly, despite her heart pounding. "He has been waiting for all of these long years for the one person who could prove himself worthy enough, and who could show real courage. He has found the one person who could stand for everything that he stood for, the person who could pass all three tests. Arthur has come back in you."

Slowly Lance absorbed what she was telling him. He could not bring himself to believe that the mighty King Arthur had come back in... *him*? Shaking his head, he looked stunned as he turned away from her.

"No, you must be wrong. I'm nowhere near brave enough. I'm a coward who always runs away from even the slightest hint of trouble. I can't possibly be anything like good enough."

"You have shown your strengths on so many occasions." Gwyn continued to smile softly. "And we've all been willing you to succeed, right from the very first moment when we saw you among that group of people you were with. You are the first person in a long time to embrace everything that you have been told here. You have resisted temptation on three occasions, and you have shown the courage that was needed to stand up to the person you believed to be King Arthur when you judged him to be wrong. You could not have possibly known that that person was in fact Morgan, attempting to deceive you. She tried to weave her magic over you, but you stuck with the ideal of everything that King Arthur truly stands for. She believed that you were weak and vulnerable, and you proved how wrong she was."

Times had changed since King Arthur had actually walked in this world. The days of the sword had passed a long time ago, and King Arthur was well aware of that. He knew that he would now have to show his courage in other ways; the same way that Lance himself had shown courage. The moment when he had accepted the chain and the light had blinded him was the moment when King Arthur had joined forces with him. He and King Arthur were now one and the same, and always would be.

"I can't do it." Lance shook his head as he began to panic. "I can't live up to the legend. The only thing I'll do is let him down."

"You won't let him down, Lance. You'll do Arthur proud. You already have with the way that you've proved yourself. This transitional period as you unite will feel awkward. Once you have accepted your destiny, though, it'll be so much easier to live with."

Lance continued to stare at the ground. Surely it could not be possible… could it? Could he and the mighty King Arthur really be as one? It couldn't be true, and yet it could explain why he had been feeling so different since that meeting with Arthur. He had assumed that it had simply been a reaction to having been in the presence of the great man. With Gwyn saying nothing, he had time to take in what she had just said. To accept it completely, though, was going to take a lot longer.

"You need time to adjust, just like I did when it happened to me." Gwyn pulled out the necklace that she was wearing from beneath her jumper. "This has been in my family for many generations. It's been a tradition for it to be passed down from mother to daughter. My mother brought me here a few months before she died, as though she knew that something was going to happen to her. When Mum hung this around my neck, like Arthur hung his chain around yours, the same thing that happened to you happened to me. Guinevere was lucky. She and Arthur had two children, a son and a daughter. Unlike Arthur, she had the opportunity to pass her necklace to her daughter before she retreated to that nunnery and died."

Lance was gazing intently at the necklace, saying nothing for what felt like an eternity before speaking.

"That once belonged to Guinevere?"

"You won't tell anyone, will you? If anyone else ever finds out it'll be taken away from me. The experts will want to test it for authenticity before declaring that it's priceless and locking it away in some dusty museum for safekeeping. If they do that, they'll trap Guinevere in an airless vault until the end of all time. She belongs out here. Please promise that you won't say a word."

"I promise." Lance smiled quietly and kindly as a sudden sense of calm spread right through him. "After all, if they find out about your necklace, they'll also find out about this chain. They'll both be trapped for all time, then."

Gwyn gazed at him before looking away again. She appeared to be troubled, as if she were doubting her decision to tell him anything at all. Lance watched her carefully for a few moments; then licked his lips and summoned up the courage to speak.

"If your necklace originally came from Guinevere and my chain was given to me by King Arthur, does that mean that we also belong with each other?"

Gwyn could not look him in the eye. She could only bow her head and nod as she closed her eyes and apologized.

"So I'm meant to see you again after all," Lance stated, "and there's no need for you to be sorry. I'm glad. There's nothing I can think of that I could possibly want more. I was hoping that I'd be able to see you again, like I did the other night. I was hoping that King Arthur would let me do that, and now I know that there's nothing to stop me from being able to."

Gwyn smiled nervously as she gazed at him. She had been waiting for this moment for so long – for the reunion of King Arthur and Guinevere in this world. She had hoped beyond all hope from the very first moment that she had seen him; that he would be the one to release Arthur from the spell that had been cast over him. Now that it had happened, however, it was actually scaring her. She did not know what to expect, and no longer felt in control of the events that were about to take place. All that she knew was that they were destined to play out the legend of Arthur and Guinevere in today's modern world, and she had no way of knowing how it would all turn out.

Chapter 29

Lance opened the door to his apartment; then moved to one side and waited for Gwyn to step inside. Gwyn hesitated as she hovered in the doorway, before moving forwards and looking about the hallway as Lance followed her and quickly closed the door behind them. He ushered her through to the living room and dropped his keys onto the small side table before taking her coat from her. Draping it over the back of the settee, he disappeared into the kitchen to make some coffee.

Left alone, Gwyn looked about the room. She had been to this apartment once before, though she could remember none of it. Back then she had been too distracted to notice anything; consumed by her desire to explain to Lance what had happened at Avalon. Now she was crossing over to the row of framed photographs that were standing on the shelf. Curiosity had taken hold, encouraging her to pick one up and look at it more closely. Behind her, Lance leaned against the doorframe leading to the kitchen. He was smiling fondly as he watched her; a confidence filling him that came with the knowledge that she did not realize that he was standing there.

They had done so much together over the past few weeks. Most of their time had been spent sitting at Avalon, but they had gone out for dinner on several occasions, and to the cinema. Tonight they had been to the theatre. Gwyn was wearing a full-length sleeveless black dress, her hair hanging loosely down her back as far as her slender waist. As ever, she was wearing the necklace that Lance always found himself being attracted to. Their relationship so far had continued to be one of simple friendship, both being wary of taking the next step despite the Petersons having at last backed down and agreed to an out-of-court settlement. Tonight, though, the atmosphere was definitely feeling different.

Lance continued to gaze at Gwyn until he heard the kettle come to a boil. She looked stunning in that dress – regal, even. All that she needed was a crown. But then, if she really was a direct descendant of Arthur and Guinevere... And Gwyn's likeness to the queen was uncanny, as though enforcing the belief that that connection was true.

Reluctantly tearing himself away, Lance quickly made the coffee and joined Gwyn in the living room. Still looking at the same photograph, she glanced round at him as he appeared beside her and asked him where the house in the picture was located. With the subtle scent of her perfume filling the air, Lance was finding it almost impossible to concentrate. Gwyn was distracting him too much, not that she knew of the effect that she was having on him. Trying to pull himself together, Lance quickly looked at the photograph.

"It's our home in the hills outside Boston," he told her, "where we usually spend some weekends and our vacations. My parents own an apartment in Boston, too. That's where we stay during the week, as it's more convenient for work. My parents own this apartment as well – they bought it so I'd have somewhere to live while I'm here."

"I suppose you'll be going back there soon?" Gwyn continued to stare at the photograph. "Did you not tell me once that you're only here for a year?"

Lance swallowed as he hesitated. He did not want to think about that. Now that Gwyn had mentioned the unpleasant truth, though, the harsh reality that was his life hit him like a sledgehammer, and he did not want to go back and leave her behind.

"Come with me," he said, Gwyn quick to look round at him. "When I go back, come with me. If you think you could leave Avalon behind, that is."

Gwyn eventually looked away as Lance spoke on. He realized how much she would be sacrificing if she did leave Avalon. That was not the reason why she had hesitated, though.

"Lance, if you had asked me before, I would have given up Avalon for you," she said. "I won't be giving it up if I go to America with you, though. Avalon will follow me, and will move across the ocean with me. I wouldn't be leaving it behind. That is not the reason why I can't go over there with you. I don't possess a passport."

"That's not a problem." Lance relaxed and smiled as he handed her a mug of coffee while guiding her over to the settee. "We'll get you one. Or, if you'd rather, I could always apply for permission to live and work here."

Gwyn gazed at him in surprise as she sat down. That was an awful lot for her to ask of him, and she was not certain that his father would ever agree to let him settle here. She had met his father, albeit briefly, and had realized what he was really like. She couldn't expect Lance to plead with his father just so that she could stay here. Lance was the one who had far more to lose. Lance smiled again as he sat down beside her.

"Will you marry me?" he suddenly asked.

Gwyn stared at him in disbelief. After all these months of being just friends and spending time getting to know each other, this felt very sudden. Lance could not be more certain that this was what he wanted, though. He would not be able to bear it if she turned him down now. He had never felt so sure of anything in his entire life. He wanted to spend the rest of his life with her. He never wanted to be parted from her side, not even for the briefest of moments, and right now, he was willing her to accept him.

After what felt like a lifetime, Gwyn smiled. How could she possibly turn him down? After all the months that she had spent willing him to pass the tests that had been set so that she could be with him, she was not going to turn her back on him now. Lance smiled broadly; then he tentatively reached across and kissed her. Gwyn had agreed to marry him and become his wife.

Lance pulled back a little. Hesitating, he kissed her again before asking her to stay with him tonight. Lance gazed directly into her eyes, and Gwyn was unable to do anything but stare back at him. Lance was pleading with her to stay. He did not think that he could bear to be apart from her for any longer.

Gwyn swallowed as she tore her eyes away from his and looked down at her hands. This time he was asking an awful lot of her, and wanting her to take an enormous step. What he was asking of her was new to her. It was something that she had never experienced before, and it was frightening. This time she had no idea what to expect or what she was supposed to do.

Lance continued to gaze at her as he promised to take care of her. He would show her what to do, while not expecting too much of her. As Gwyn looked back at him, her trepidation was clear to see. Her mind was racing, and she swallowed as Lance reached across and kissed her once more. This time his chain became entangled in Gwyn's necklace, their faces held close while Lance fumbled to free them. Still feeling nervous, Gwyn looked upon this as a message from the mighty king and his queen. Swallowing, she nervously gave in as Lance finally separated the necklace and chain. He smiled encouragingly, and felt Gwyn's hand tremble as he took hold of it. Then he turned off the light as he led her out of the room. Tonight was going to be a night that they would both remember.

With two mugs of coffee in his hands, Lance looked disappointed upon finding Gwyn standing by the living room window. She had got up and dressed as soon as he had left his bedroom to make the coffee, and had followed him as far as the living room. Now that he was joining her again, Lance's expression was making her feel guilty. She wanted to return home, though, in case Gareth decided to call in on her. The last thing that she wanted to face right now was his reaction when he found out about her and Lance. Right now, she could not risk upsetting him. She couldn't do that until she had a passport.

Lance smiled and kissed her as he handed her a mug of coffee. He would take her home, if that was what she really wanted. Then he slid an arm around her so that he could sympathize with and comfort her, kissing the side of her head before reluctantly letting her go. Leaving his mug of coffee on the coffee table, he left the room so that he could dress in jeans and a sweatshirt. He knew that he had to do as she wished, no matter how much he wanted her to stay here with him. The reality was that this was the only way in which he could keep hold of her and ensure that he did not drive her away. Life would be perfect if it was not for Gareth. Gwyn, however, was the one who knew him the best. Lance could do nothing right now but accept her decision and drive her home.

The weather outside was dull and windy, making Gwyn huddle into her coat as Lance opened the car door for her. She climbed in eagerly, glad to shelter from the cold wind. She would be lying if she claimed that she had not eventually enjoyed the previous night. Lance had proven to be so kind and gentle, and he had given her the time that she needed to settle her nerves. Her only regret now was the prospect of having to face Gareth. She could easily predict what he was likely to say, and she had an awful feeling that he would be far from pleased.

Lance started the engine; then pulled on his seatbelt before driving away from the apartment. Gwyn was quiet, and Lance was too preoccupied with his thoughts to notice. She had agreed to marry him, and to spend the rest of her life by his side. At least his mother would be pleased. There was no doubting that she was going to welcome the person sitting in this car with him into the family with open arms. There was also, however, no doubting that his father's reaction was likely to be the complete opposite.

A familiar, stone-built house eventually came into sight as they followed the dirt track that they had turned on to. Even from this distance, they could immediately recognize the car that was parked outside. Gareth was already here, and would undoubtedly be waiting for an explanation. Gwyn's fears were already increasing. Neither of them had expected this, and as she was still wearing her evening dress, she could not deny that she hadn't returned home the previous night.

Lance pulled up alongside Gareth's car and turned off the engine. He was not going to desert Gwyn now. He was not going to abandon her while she faced her brother alone. This time he was determined to stand beside the woman he loved, no matter what the consequences were to be. With Gareth already emerging from the house, Lance watched him carefully as he began to stride towards them.

"If the worst is going to happen," Lance told Gwyn, "then I'll look after you. If Gareth is going to be truly awful to you, then I'll take you back with me to the apartment."

The pair took a deep breath before climbing out of the car. Gareth's eyes were fiery with rage, as he immediately demanded an explanation. He gave them no chance to reply, however, instead accusing Gwyn of staying with Lance the night before.

"How could you?" he demanded. "You've done nothing but bring shame on our parents. What do you think they'd have said if they were still alive? I can see exactly what you've both been doing. I'm disappointed in you, Gwyn. I'm disappointed and ashamed of you. I mean, with a Yank of all people, too—"

"Don't you dare!" Gwyn retaliated at last. "Say what you like about me. I'll take it all. But one thing I will not do is hear a single bad word said about Lance. He's a decent man, and a true gentleman who you could learn so much from. What's more, he's asked me to marry him, and I've accepted, so you'll just have to get used to it."

Gareth's expression changed from disbelief to horror as her words sank in. That horror was then replaced with disgust, Gareth almost trembling with anger as he stared at her with disdain. With his voice as cold as ice, he told her to pack her belongings and leave. To think that, after all of the sacrifices he had made and everything that he had done for her, this was how she was now repaying him. The mere sight of her repulsed him, and he never wanted to see her again.

Gwyn quickly gave up trying to reason with Gareth. With his mind made up, he was going to listen to nothing. Looking numb with shock, she conceded defeat as she disappeared into the house. Gareth watched her walk along the garden path and step through the doorway; then turned on Lance.

"I presume that you believe that you've been incredibly clever," he accused. "What do you think gives you the right to behave like some knight in shining armour and take my sister away from me?"

"You're the one who is throwing your sister out," Lance pointed out. A quiet confidence had suddenly taken hold of him, and Lance knew that King Arthur was here, and was supporting him.

"I had no choice," Gareth claimed. "I had to after you dared to desecrate her. She belongs here. Now you want to take her over to America with you, and I'll never see my sister again."

"If Gwyn does not want to move to Boston," Lance said, remaining calm, "then I'm not going to force her to. This is not about me. This is all about what Gwyn wants. I'd never make her do anything that she doesn't want to do. You are the one who is forcing her away from you."

"You really think that you know it all, don't you," Gareth remarked sarcastically. "You think that I don't know my own sister? I'm not to blame for any of this. All of this is your fault. If you hadn't come here, my sister would still be happy and would not have had her mind poisoned by you. Well, just so that you know, I'll make sure that you get nothing from my family. Everything that belongs here is going to remain here, that I can guarantee. Then we'll see how long it takes for my sister to come crawling back to where she really belongs."

Bitter hostility was clearly showing in his eyes as Gareth warned Lance to make the most of the time that he would have with his sister. Gareth believed that that time would be short. Gwyn would quickly realize the mistake she had made, and she would then come crawling back. Gareth glared at Lance for a moment or two longer; then he turned, marched back into the house and slammed the door shut behind him. Within moments, he could be heard arguing fiercely with Gwyn.

Still sensing Arthur and Guinevere's presence, Lance approached the closed door; then stopped when it suddenly opened again. Gwyn was holding a canvas bag in each hand as she stepped back outside. She had been feeling strangely different since staying with Lance last night. She had finally dared to take the step that she had been dreading, and she had realized afterwards that she would never feel the same way again. Her naïve innocence had gone, instead replaced with a sensation in her stomach that told her that she had become a grown woman. Her childish purity had been lost forever, and now Gareth's reaction was doing nothing to comfort her. Instead he was making her feel dirty and worthless, and leading her to believe that she had just committed the worst possible sin.

Gareth left the rest of Gwyn's belongings in two boxes on the front path; then slammed the door shut again. Lance and Gwyn jumped a little, both staring at the firmly closed door before Lance took one of the bags from her, slid a comforting arm around her and guided her back to the car. He couldn't see any point in them hanging around here any longer today. Maybe, once her brother had calmed down, they could try to talk to him again. For now, though, Lance was going to take Gwyn back to the apartment. He had meant every word that he had said. He was going to look after her.

Lance believed that Gwyn had every right to feel distraught. She had every right to cry. What Gareth had just done to her was unforgivable. He could not justify expecting her to give up on any life for herself so that she could be here on the odd occasion when he might need her. Lance could appreciate what Gareth had done for her after their parents had died, but what he was now expecting in return far exceeded that. He certainly did not deserve her as a sister. Wise enough to keep his thoughts to himself, Lance knew that Gwyn did not need his lecture right now.

Gwyn kept her eyes firmly on the ground in front of her feet as Lance guided her back up to his apartment. Unable to stop weeping, she could only hope and pray that no-one else noticed as they made their way to the apartment. Glad to step through the doorway, she apologized for having become such a burden to him. There was nothing that she could offer him, and she had no way of paying him back for his kindness at taking her in like this

Lance gathered her up in his arms and hugged her. She had once offered him a place to stay if ever he had needed it, and that was something he would never forget. And in any case, she was not offering him nothing, as she claimed. She had agreed to be his wife, and so it was now time for her to let him look after her and give her the support that she so obviously needed right now. Right here, beside him, would be her home.

"Why don't you have a shower while I fetch your boxes from the car?" he suggested.

Lance watched as she disappeared into the bathroom, and then he picked up his keys and mobile phone and let himself back out of the apartment. He needed someone to turn to for help, and for the first time in his life he could only think of his mother.

When he called her, she was caught by surprise at his explanation. Lance was asking for her help. He was hoping that she would fly back over and help them work out what they were going to do next. He really did not know how to deal with this situation. With Arthur and Guinevere appearing to have deserted them, he really needed his mother's help to think more clearly and hopefully sort this mess out.

Chapter 30

Two days had passed since Gwyn's confrontation with her brother, and she had not set foot out of the apartment since. Lance had done everything that he could to support her, as he had remained with her for the whole time. Feeling wretched and like a burden to him, she had been unable to stop crying. Gareth had made it perfectly clear that she could not return to the familiarity of her old life, though. She had no-one else she could turn to for help, and nowhere else to go.

Gwyn quickly looked round at Lance when they heard the doorbell ring. She looked terrified. They both knew who would be standing at the door, waiting to be let in. Lance smiled encouragingly, hoping that she would not see how nervous he was himself. He squeezed her hand gently, and then he was up on his feet and disappearing out of the room. Nervously wringing her hands, Gwyn moved across to the window and watched as three people appeared in the doorway. Lance's mother was the first who came into view, Gwyn gazing at her as tears welled up in her eyes and she began to apologize.

"Oh, you poor child!" Mrs Brookes hurried across the room and gathered Gwyn up in her arms. "What has that brother of yours done to you? You've done nothing wrong, and certainly nothing that you need to apologize for. Gareth has just shown how completely callous and uncaring he is. We'll look after you and make sure that you are all right."

The collection of embroideries that Gwyn's mother had designed and stitched were the only things that Gwyn had wanted to keep. Apart from the necklace that was still hanging around her neck, they were the only reminder that she had of a happy and carefree childhood. They meant nothing to Gareth, and yet he had refused to let his sister keep them. Instead, in his spite, he had kept them to use as a lure to tempt her back. He really believed that that simple action would be enough to force her to give up on the life with Lance that she wanted and return to a life of eternal servitude to him.

Gwyn began to weep again. If she were truly honest, she would have to admit that that was what hurt her the most. She had meant what she said when Lance had asked her to move to America with him: she would have been more than prepared to not only give up the only life that she had ever known, but to give up Avalon itself. Gareth's refusal to let her keep her mother's embroideries had devastated her, though. She was not sure that she could let that collection go.

Lance said nothing as he watched from the living room doorway. He still had no idea what to say to help Gwyn recover. He was at a complete loss. Nudged in the arm, Lance looked round at his father, who was standing beside him. Mr Brookes nodded his head; then led the way through to the kitchen. Lance looked back at Gwyn, hesitating, and then he followed his father. Two days ago he could not have been happier. Then they had had that confrontation with Gareth, and Gwyn had been completely distraught ever since. Nothing that he had tried to say or do had comforted or cheered her up. He had actually been relieved when his mother had arrived, but now that meant that he also had to face his father.

Mr Brookes waited impatiently by the door between the kitchen and living room, closing it firmly once Lance had stepped through to the kitchen. Then he looked at his son for what felt like an eternity before passing Lance as he crossed the room and switched the kettle on.

"She's very plain to look at, isn't she?" Blake Brookes remarked as he broke the tense silence. "And she has no money behind her to offer to us. You've really excelled yourself this time. What were you thinking of, asking her to marry you? For some reason, though, your mother appears to like her, so I obviously have no choice but to accept her into the family. You should have consulted me before you proposed."

Lance remained silent, his father's words somehow making him feel ashamed. He did not believe that Gwyn was plain, though – far from it. She was far more attractive than Cindy Peterson could ever hope to be. That was something that his father would never be capable of seeing. Lance also did not care about Gwyn not having a vast fortune to her name. What she did have was something that was far more valuable, and that too was something that his father would never be able to understand.

"Just so you know," Mr Brookes continued, "I think her brother was wrong to throw her out. What kind of world does he live in, for heaven's sake? It's not as though you'd taken advantage and not proposed to the girl. But as he *has* thrown her out and we've been forced to take her in, we're going to have to make the best of the situation, I suppose. If you're determined to marry the girl then you'd better make an honest woman out of her sooner rather than later. Have you got her an engagement ring yet?"

Lance shook his head. Gwyn was still trying to come to terms with what her brother had done to her, and so had not wanted to go anywhere. Now it appeared as though they also had his father's disapproval to contend with. Why had he insisted upon coming over as well? He undoubtedly wanted to assume complete control over the situation. He was hardly diplomatic, though, and Lance wished that his father had left them to sort this out by themselves. Wanting to pluck up the courage to say something, he could only take the two mugs of coffee that his father was handing to him.

"Take her to the jewellers' first thing tomorrow morning," Mr Brookes told him, "and then we'll leave her with your mother while we go to the office so we can actually get some work done. That is what you're here for, after all. Maybe your mother will be able to do something with her to make her look more presentable, like a decent haircut for a start. You can't possibly take her to Boston looking like she does at the moment."

Lance really wanted to defend Gwyn by telling his father that she was worth a million Cindy Petersons. King Arthur was still deserting him, though, and his own courage had completely drained out of him. All that he could do was say nothing and stand by helplessly while his father said exactly what he thought. Right now was definitely not the time to tell his father that they might not want to live in Boston.

Mr Brookes had picked up the other two mugs of coffee and was now leading the way back into the living room. Mrs Brookes was still trying to comfort Gwyn, the pair now sitting on the settee. Though Gwyn was not actually weeping at the moment, she was still looking numb and shocked over what had happened to her. She was staring into space and saying nothing, looking up only when a mug of coffee appeared in front of her.

Lance was smiling nervously down at her as he offered her the drink, waiting until she had taken the mug from him before sitting down beside her and automatically sliding a comforting arm around her.

Mrs Brookes, in contrast, glared up at her husband as she took the mug of coffee that he was handing to her. She had heard every word that he had just said to Lance, and she knew that Gwyn had to have heard them too. Now he was daring to act as though he believed that he had done nothing wrong as he made polite conversation.

Gwyn was still saying nothing as she absentmindedly swallowed a mouth full of coffee in a desperate bid to steady her nerves. She was numb, feeling no emotion at all. She had been truly devastated by Gareth's words and actions. Surely what she and Lance had done had not been that horrific? They did, after all, want to spend the rest of their lives together. Surely Lance being American could not be that bad?

Night had fallen when Lance guided Gwyn into his bedroom. Gwyn hesitated in the hallway, not knowing whether his parents would approve or not. Even though they had passed no comment at all on the subject, she remained nervous. Lance closed the door behind them; then he guided her across to the bed so that they could sit in the darkness while he spent a long time assuring her that everything would be all right.

"Take no notice of what my father says," he said. "He knows nothing. He's only showing his ignorance. My mother adores you, and that's all that matters. She'll not hear a bad word said against you."

Knowing that Lance was being forced to leave her with his mother in the morning did not help Gwyn fall asleep. She had barely slept at all since Lance had brought her back here. She knew that she should be feeling really happy to be here with him, but instead she had been miserable and unable to do anything but cry. Deep down, she knew that none of this was her fault, and that she had done nothing wrong. Guinevere's constant assurances were beginning to convince her of that. Gareth's unreasonable behaviour had upset her, though, and had affected her a lot more than she had thought it would. Eventually she forced a weak smile and settled down to sleep.

Gwyn was standing on the pavement as Mrs Brookes pulled the jewellers' shop door shut. She was wearing a ring that shone brightly in the sunlight. Gwyn was numb, unable to believe how much the ring had cost, and now she was also feeling self-conscious, certain that the whole world was staring at the ring that she was wearing.

Lance put an arm around her as he quickly hugged and kissed her before reluctantly letting her go again. His father was waiting impatiently for him. He wanted to get to the office, where there was work to do that could not be put off any longer. Lance was headed away along the pavement, his father towering beside him. Gwyn watched them go, noticing now how Lance's hair had been forced into the same style as his father's.

"Come on, then." Mrs Brookes put an arm around Gwyn and guided her away. "First we need to get you a replacement birth certificate. Then we need to get a passport application and some photographs. Then we can go shopping and get you a whole new wardrobe. How much fun will that be?"

Gwyn smiled nervously. There was no denying that, as far as Mrs Brookes was concerned, they were about to have the time of their lives as they indulged in her future mother-in-law's favourite pastime.

Laden down with bags, Mrs Brookes struggled to push the key into the lock of the apartment. She was doggedly refusing to put anything down, instead fumbling for a few moments before managing to push the door open and struggle inside. Gwyn followed her, shutting the door while Mrs Brookes headed for the living room. Dropping the key onto the side table, Mrs Brookes finally put the bags that she was carrying down on the armchair before disappearing into the kitchen. It was time, she decided, for a coffee. They had, she believed, definitely earned it.

Mrs Brookes returned to the living room, where Gwyn was still staring at the mountain of bags that were on the armchair. She looked dazed, having never known so many new clothes before. Everything that she had ever possessed in the past had either been second-hand or made by herself.

"This is nothing more than you deserve." Mrs Brookes smiled warmly as she handed her a mug of coffee and put an arm around her. "After everything that you've done for Lance, this is the least that we can do for you. Besides, you're very nearly one of the family now. You have a whole new life to look forward to."

Gwyn sat down on the settee and sipped her coffee as she stared at the partly-finished embroidery that she had left on the coffee table. It was her latest design, the one that she had been working on when Gareth had so callously thrown her out. Then yesterday, Lance's father had dismissed it as a work of complete fantasy, and now she had no incentive to continue. Absentmindedly staring at it, she suddenly caught her breath and looked at Mrs Brookes.

"What is it?" Nancy Brookes looked concerned. "What's wrong?"

Gwyn's hands were shaking as her fingers wrapped around her mug.

"Nothing is wrong," she said. "I've just had a thought. As far as Gareth is concerned, I no longer exist. If that's the case, then I won't be able to supply him with any new designs. I'll be able to give those designs to someone else instead. Someone like you, if you're still interested."

Mrs Brookes grinned broadly as she gazed at Gwyn. Gareth really had not thought his actions through properly. And if this was what Gwyn really wanted, then maybe she would be able to open a shop in Boston after all. Suddenly filled with a new-found ambition and energy, Gwyn put down her mug and pulled out her pencil and graph paper. She was going to need time to come up with enough new designs for Mrs Brookes. She needed to start with small and simple designs to give Lance's mother something to begin with. Now focused and resolute, Gwyn began to draw. She had work to do.

Chapter 31

Gwyn looked stunned. She had summoned the courage to come here and face Gareth so that she could tell him in person that she was no longer going to supply him with new designs. Laura, however, had just told her that Gareth was not here. Gwyn had missed him by a matter of minutes. He had gone over to Gwyn's house, and he had taken a woman with him. Suddenly snapping back to reality, Gwyn forced a brave smile as she looked across at Laura.

"It doesn't matter," she claimed, "I'll catch him another time. Thanks for signing my passport application and photograph."

Laura watched as Gwyn turned to leave. "I'm really sorry, Gwyn," Laura dared to speak out while Gareth was not present to hear her, "I've no idea what's got into that brother of yours. It's not as though he hasn't always had a whole string of women himself, and rarely just one at a time. You've done nothing wrong, and Lance appears to be a really nice person, too. Gareth needs his head testing. I'm going to miss you, though it does sound very exciting. I can guarantee that you'll do really well."

Gwyn smiled sadly as she thanked Laura again before turning towards the door for a second time. Laura, however, was speaking again, once again stopping Gwyn from leaving just yet.

"Why don't you go and see the solicitor," Laura suggested, "and take a look at your parents' will? I know for a fact that they made one."

Gwyn gazed at her; then eventually nodded and finally left the shop. She crossed the road and climbed into the waiting car next to Mrs Brookes. This was the very space where Lance and his father had sat and watched the shop for a while to see how busy it was before Mr Brookes had made his way over yesterday. Somehow he had succeeded in getting all of the embroideries off Gareth. Lance had presented them to Gwyn later that evening, making her weep tears of joy. She wasn't stupid, though; she knew that Gareth would never hand them over for nothing. The vast sum of money that Mr Brookes had been forced to pay for them, however, was to remain a closely guarded secret.

"What's wrong?" Mrs Brookes asked, noting the dazed expression on Gwyn's face.

"Gareth isn't here, and to think that he dared to take the moral high ground with me. How dare he, after what I've just learned? Would you mind if I just make another call?"

Gwyn was clearly feeling both indignant and offended, and Mrs Brookes watched as she climbed back out of the car and hurried away up the narrow street. Where she was heading to and how long she would be, Mrs Brookes had no idea. Time dragged by slowly, and Lance's mother was relieved when she eventually saw Gwyn hurrying back.

"Sorry I was so long." Gwyn sounded a little breathless as she climbed back into the car. "I ended up making two calls."

She needed to go nowhere else, except back to the office so that she could see Lance and his father. Gwyn hesitated, waiting until Graham had pulled away from the kerb and was heading back towards Bristol before continuing. She then opened the envelope that she was holding and pulled out the contents. She doubted that Mrs Brookes would believe what she was about to show her. Gwyn was still finding it almost impossible to take in herself.

Mrs Brookes took the copy of the will that Gwyn was offering her and read it through. Gwyn waited impatiently for her to finish, and nodded when Mrs Brookes looked back at her. It was true. Her parents had left Gareth a lump sum of money – money that had been paid to him three months after their parents had died. Everything else had been left to her. The shop and the embroideries, and even the house that Gareth had thrown her out of, were rightfully hers. Lance's father had just paid Gwyn's brother heaven knows how much money for something that Gareth had no claim over.

There was more. Gwyn handed the rest of the paperwork to Mrs Brookes, except for one small piece of paper, as she continued to explain. Her second call had been to the accountants in charge of the family finances. They had given her the latest set of accounts for the shop. Gareth had not only paid himself a decent wage for managing the shop, but he had also creamed off all of the profits over the last six years and had them paid into a separate account that was solely in his name. The accountants had checked the past and present records, and had written down how much profit Gareth had awarded himself in total.

Gwyn handed over the last piece of paper. Mrs Brookes stared at it, finding it impossible to take it all in. The enormity of the situation was slowly sinking in. For the last six years, Gareth had been cheating his own sister out of everything that was rightfully hers. He had also callously thrown her out with nothing while fully intending and expecting to keep it all for himself. This was why Gwyn was looking so dazed and pale. Anger quickly rose up inside Lance's mother. Now they could not get back to Bristol quickly enough, Lance and his father looking up in surprise when she burst into the office and dropped the paperwork onto the table in front of them.

"Just take a look at that," she ordered, Gwyn silently slipping into the office behind her. "Just look at what Gwyn's brother has done to her. He's taken it all from her. It all belongs to Gwyn."

Gwyn stood just inside the door and said nothing while Mr Brookes studied the will and set of accounts. He was able to take it all in quickly, and he looked up at her when he had done so, asking her if she had confronted her brother about this yet. Gwyn shook her head. Though she wanted to, she had decided to think things through properly.

Mr Brookes sat back in his chair and nodded knowingly. Lance, however, got up and crossed over to where Gwyn was standing. Mrs Brookes, meanwhile, was pushing all of the paperwork back into the envelope as she suggested that Lance and Gwyn went back to the apartment. It all needed a lot of serious thought, and was going to have to be sorted out before they moved to Boston.

Gwyn glanced at Lance, before taking the envelope and leaving the office with him. Only yesterday evening their future plans had all been worked out. Gwyn had, in fact, already made her decision before Lance and his father had got back to the apartment. She was going to marry Lance, move to Boston with him and become an American citizen. She was then going to work on producing exclusive designs for Mrs Brookes to sell in her shop. It had all been so simple and straightforward. Now, though, everything needed thinking through again. It had suddenly been made complicated.

Gwyn stopped next to the car and stared into space before looking round at Lance. She was being drawn to Avalon, and needed to go there before they returned to the apartment. Why she needed to, she did not yet know. She was just feeling compelled to go and visit the lake. Lance nodded and took the car keys from Graham. Nothing was said, nor did it need to be said. Lance knew all too well how overwhelming and compelling any urge to go to Avalon was. If that was where Gwyn needed to go, then that was where he would take her.

Gwyn left the envelope in the car when they eventually came to a stop beside a very familiar hillside. Climbing the hill, they hesitated upon reaching the wood. They did not know whether Gareth was still in the nearby house or not, and they were not interested in knowing. He was the last person they wanted to see at the moment. They stepped into the wood and made their way through the trees to reach the lake. Tranquil and quiet, the clearing was, as always, bathed in the white light that made the swirling mist glow eerily. The pair stopped when they reached a familiar spot and gazed across at the mist-shrouded island.

Lance said nothing as he stood beside Gwyn. She called out and asked what she should do.

Should she go to Boston and start a new life as she had planned, or was she supposed to stay here? She was feeling torn between the two places; between the excitement and adventure of starting afresh and her loyalty to her parents. Was she really destined to remain here and take over the shop from Gareth? And what about Lance? Could she expect him to give up everything that he had ever known?

Gwyn looked at Lance. He smiled back at her, telling her that it was her choice. If she really wanted to stay here, then he would stay here too. He would be the one who would be making the fresh start instead of her. As long as they were together then he did not care where they lived. It seemed right, though, that they had come here. Here was where they had first met, and where their bond had developed. It seemed only right that right here was where Gwyn eventually decided their future. Could they really live without Avalon? Could they start a new life in Boston and leave this magical place behind? In reality, could either of them let Avalon go?

Familiar voices were drifting over to them upon the light breeze. Arthur and Guinevere spoke to them, uttering words of wisdom as they told them that, no matter where in the world they chose to live, Arthur and Guinevere would never be far away. Through Lance and Gwyn, they too lived on. Wherever they went, Arthur and Guinevere would follow them. However, a decision could not be made until Gwyn had gone to Boston and experienced the city for herself. Only then would she truly know if she really could live there for the rest of her life in this world. Of one thing, though, they were certain: Gwyn and Lance were to remain together for the rest of their mortal lives.

Gwyn was gaining no comfort from the words that had just been spoken. Her mind remained in turmoil as she gazed across at the island. She was no closer to knowing which decision to make. There was also the added problem of what she was to do with Gareth. Their parents had obviously believed that everything would be in safer hands if left to her, so there was no denying that she was going to have to oust Gareth from the shop. That was something that she had known right from the start, and she was not looking forward to it. He was not going to go quietly, that much Gwyn could guarantee. Gareth would undoubtedly retaliate, and was likely to destroy everything that was dearest to her.

Gwyn slowly reached up and took off her necklace as she continued to stare at the island. To her, Avalon was the most sacred place in this world, and Gareth would think nothing of taking advantage by directing thousands of people here so that they could stare across at that island. In effect, he would completely destroy the place. It would no longer be a sanctuary for her. Then he would probably tell everyone that her necklace had once belonged to Guinevere.

Something unseen was urging her to return it to the lake. It was the only way in which she could protect it all. Gwyn stepped forwards; then looked back at Lance when he stopped her, offering the chain that had been hanging around his neck. He believed that they too belonged together, and that they should go back to the lake together. Gwyn gazed at him before eventually taking the chain from him and interlacing it with her necklace to prevent them from ever separating. The task complete, she offered them back to Lance. He was stronger than her, and she wanted him to throw them into the lake. He would, after all, be able to throw them further than she would.

Lance hesitated; then took the chain and necklace from her. He searched her eyes, as though seeking assurance that she really did want him to do this. Only then did he turn to face the lake and throw the chain and necklace as far as he could across the still, grey waters.

Chapter 32

Gwyn and Lance watched as the threaded jewellery flew across the water, neither of them at all surprised when a hand broke through the lake's surface. Droplets of water sparkled in the white light as they fell back into the lake, fingers quickly seizing hold of the chain and necklace as more droplets joined those that had already returned to the water. The hand paused for a few long moments; then slowly sank back down beneath the water's surface. A hushed silence fell upon the scene, Gwyn and Lance saying nothing as they watched the expanding ripples stretch out over the lake. Nothing else happened for a few more moments, and then the white light began to intensify until it blinded them, while a brisk wind sprang up from nowhere.

Gwyn and Lance had no idea what was going on, and instinctively they clutched hold of each other. Nothing could be seen in the blinding light that illuminated the whole area with an unnatural intensity. With the sound of the wind now blotting out all other sounds, they could do nothing but cling desperately onto each other as they feared being carried away and lost for all time. What they were now experiencing had been totally unexpected, and in truth neither could understand what was actually going on.

At last, after what felt like an eternity, the wind died down as the brilliant white light faded back to nothing. It took the pair a few moments for their eyes to adjust before they could look about them. There were no trees and no lake. It had all disappeared, leaving them on an open hillside that rolled on as though it had done so for centuries. Avalon had gone.

Stunned and shocked, they quickly looked round upon hearing a shriek nearby. Two people were scrambling up onto their feet and snatching up their clothes as they hastily covered themselves while shielding themselves behind the familiar car that was parked nearby. They were standing where the house that up until recently Gwyn had called home had once stood. That, too, was nowhere to be seen. Like the lake with its island and the wood, the house had also vanished.

Gwyn stared at the two people who were standing behind the car. She was still too shocked to take anything in, which gave Gareth the chance to eventually emerge from behind the car and start to walk towards his sister and Lance. Then he suddenly stopped, his expression revealing that he now realized that he had been well and truly caught out. Given their state of undress, he could not deny what he and his companion had been doing. All that he could now do was glare directly at Gwyn as he decided that his only defence was to attack her.

Gwyn, however, was gazing sadly at him as he began to shout and swear at her. Then, without saying a word, she slowly shook her head and began to walk away. There was nothing that Gwyn wanted to say to Gareth right now. Instead, with Lance walking beside her with his protective and comforting arm around her, she headed back to the car. Only when they had climbed in did Lance break the silence as he asked her if she was all right. Gwyn nodded. There was nothing that she wanted to say or do here now. It was time for them to return to Bristol.

Lance made some coffee and joined Gwyn in the living room once they were safely in the apartment. The pictures that she had drawn only yesterday were still lying on the coffee table, the colours still to be chosen. With the envelope of paperwork now lying on the table beside her drawings, Gwyn was staring into space as she sat on the settee, still trying to take in everything that had happened to her that day. It had proved to be a day filled with one revelation after another.

Gwyn took the mug of coffee that Lance offered as he appeared before her. He stared at the drawings that were scattered over the coffee table, just as they had landed when his father had casually tossed them aside as he dismissed them all as pure fantasy. Gwyn had not given him the reaction that he had been seeking, still too distracted by her expected confrontation with her brother to even hear what he had said.

"What's going on, Gwyn?" Lance suddenly asked. "I can grasp the fact that Gareth had claimed for himself what is rightfully yours, but those accounts mean nothing to me. I know that my father understood them, but to me it was just a jumble of numbers."

Gwyn put her mug down, picked up the envelope and pulled out the contents. "Gareth has claimed an official and proper wage over the last six years," she explained, "and there's nothing wrong with that. But he's also helped himself to the hundreds of thousands of pounds in profit at the same time. He's basically grabbed every last penny that he could get hold of. This number here is the amount of profit he's taken in total. And when you consider that he's left me with nothing and expected you and your parents to take me in…"

Lance stared at the row of numbers that were written on the insignificant-looking piece of paper. At the moment, he found it all too hard to take in.

"I don't know what to do now," Gwyn confessed. "I mean, yesterday everything was so simple: I was going to start from the very beginning with a fresh new life. Now everything's been turned upside down and has become complicated. And with Avalon having gone, I can't even go there to try to work things out."

"We could still go to that spot." Lance put the paper down on the coffee table. "Just because we won't be able to see it, it doesn't mean that it's not there. It'll always be there to us."

"Avalon will be wherever we want it to be," Gwyn smiled weakly as she reminded him. "It won't matter where in the world we decide to settle – Avalon will always be with us. The problem I have now is the shop. Laura has always been so supportive, and I'll feel awful if after everything that she's done for me, I just give up and move away. Why did Gareth have to be out? If he'd been there, then none of this would have happened."

"Well, maybe we're supposed to stay here," Lance suggested. "To be honest, I've felt more at home here than I've ever felt in Boston. And I'm not just saying that – I've felt more of a part of things here. Not only has everyone made me feel welcome, but I feel valued for who I really am. Perhaps you should just do one thing at a time and work out what you're going to do about Gareth. He is still your brother, after all."

Brother or not, Gareth was not going to be in the shop for much longer. Gwyn could not forgive him for what he had done. She had had no idea that Avalon would disappear when they returned the necklace and chain to the lake. She had instinctively known that it was the only way to protect Avalon, but she had not known that they would also inadvertently expose Gareth for what he really was. He had had no excuse and no explanation. It had given her the opportunity to look him in the eye and walk away with her head held high, secure in the knowledge that he had been a total hypocrite. Right now she owed him nothing. After the way Gareth had behaved, it would be the easiest decision in the world to treat him in the same way that he had treated her. Tomorrow she was going to have to go over to Glastonbury and throw him out, as he had thrown her out. She was also going to demand that he repaid the money that he had taken from Lance's father in exchange for the embroideries.

Lance's parents arrived at the end of the afternoon, Mrs Brookes joining Gwyn in the kitchen as she checked how dinner was cooking. Gwyn was still numb with shock as she told Lance's mother what had happened at Avalon. One thing she had realized since returning home was that there was nothing now to stop Mrs Brookes from opening a shop with all of their designs.

The two women returned to the living room with the coffee that had been made, Gwyn sitting down as she announced that she wanted to return to the shop in Glastonbury in the morning. To prevent Gareth from causing any damage, she wanted to evict him as soon as possible. She did not want to think about what he was capable of, especially after they had caught him out today.

"You're not going over on your own," Lance told her, feeling unusually emboldened.

"We'll all go," Mr Brookes decided.

Gwyn did not argue. She was feeling relieved, glad even, that she would have their support. It would make a difficult task that little bit easier, although she was still not looking forward to the task. She knew only too well what Gareth would be like, and the mere thought of it filled her with dread.

"This is going to make things a little bit more difficult, isn't it," Mrs Brookes remarked as she sat down beside Gwyn, "having the shop to sort out before you join us in Boston? It'll be a shame, you having to sell it."

"I don't see why she has to sell," Mr Brookes spoke up. "It'll provide her with a pretty decent source of income, from what I can remember. She'll earn much more if she keeps it."

Gwyn looked down at her mug, unable to bring herself to admit that indeed she didn't want to sell. Lance, too, remained quiet, his father's comments diverting attention away from their tension. Looking at each other, Gwyn and Lance still said nothing. Mr Brookes was, as always, taking charge and giving no consideration to anyone else's thoughts. Gwyn, it now appeared, was not the penniless tramp that he had believed her to be after all. She was worth an almost respectable amount of money, and with his guidance, she could easily be worth so much more. Maybe Lance had not made such a monumental mistake after all.

Chapter 33

Gareth glared at the small group as he dared any one of them to object. He wanted to speak to his sister, and to her alone. Gwyn reluctantly relented. It would make no difference. Too much had happened recently for her to change her mind now. She knew that if she let him speak to her, though, he would not be able to accuse her of not giving him a chance. She was at least giving him that, despite Gareth having refused to give her any such opportunity. Gwyn moved through to the next room, Gareth quickly closing the door behind them.

"Why are you doing this, Gwyn?" he asked. "I'm your brother. Surely that has to amount to something. They've put you up to this, haven't they? They're obviously not content with stealing you away from me—"

"Stop it, Gareth," Gwyn quickly cut in, "this has nothing to do with Lance or his parents. I've seen what you've been doing over the last six years. You knew that this shop had been left to me, didn't you? That's the only reason why you agreed to look after me after Mum and Dad died, isn't it? It's why you found me that house and encouraged me to stay over there. You wanted to keep me out of the way so that I only knew what you wanted me to know."

"You were always the favourite. I was left with nothing."

"That's not true." Gwyn gazed sadly at him. "Mum and Dad made sure that you would be all right. You got the money they left you; but then you became greedy. Once you saw how profitable the shop was, you wanted it all for yourself. You only needed to accept Lance. You couldn't do that, though, could you? You wanted to keep me hidden away so that I could continue providing you with the lifestyle that you had created for yourself, and you preferred to throw me out and leave me with nothing when you realized how close Lance and I had become."

"He's an American, Gwyn, and that's all it needs for me to despise him. Not only that, but he's planning on taking you back to America with him. He's stealing you away from me. You deserve someone far better than him. There's got to be someone who is far more worthy of you."

Gareth realized his mistake when he noticed the way that Gwyn was gazing at him. It was too late now, though – he could not take back the words that had just been spoken. Gwyn's quiet insistence that she wanted him to leave and give all of this up had made him increasingly irrational. He had just blurted out the words that should have remained unspoken.

"Lance is looked upon as more than worthy enough by *King Arthur*, Gareth," Gwyn told him. "He passed all three of the tests that Morgan set, and he's revealed his true strength and courage. He's accepted Arthur and freed the king, allowing Arthur to return to this world. King Arthur is living on again through Lance. Where Lance has come from is obviously of no importance."

Gareth could only listen as Gwyn quietly talked on. She and Lance were going to get married this summer. They were going to honeymoon in Boston, though they did not yet know whether they wanted to settle there. Whether they did or not, however, she was still going to supply this shop with new designs. Gareth could have been a part of it all, if only he had accepted Lance. Because he could not, because of his unreasonable behaviour, she had been left with no choice but to make him leave. He had brought all of this upon himself, and there was no-one else whom he could justifiably blame.

Gareth began to object again, but was stopped by his sister. She had come here yesterday to tell him that she was no longer going to supply him with new designs. He had decided that she no longer existed, so she had decided to supply Lance's mother instead to thank her for the way they had taken her in. It was the only thing that she believed she was able to offer them. She would still be none the wiser if he had been here as he was supposed to have been, but there was nothing more that could be said now. Gwyn wanted him out, and she wanted him out right now.

Gwyn wanted to say nothing else. Gareth could say what he liked; it would make no difference. Her mind had been made up. She now let herself out of the sparsely-furnished room and rejoined Lance and his parents in the office. Gareth watched her go as he finally realized that he really did have no choice but to do as she had told him. It was, after all, only what he had done to her. With his mouth set firmly in a hard line, Gareth made his way up to the flat above the shop so that he could pack his belongings.

Gwyn stared down at the floor in front of her after watching her brother leave the room. She could not deny that she was hating every moment of this. After all, Gareth was still her brother, and nothing could possibly change that. She was burning hot with embarrassment, forcing a smile as Lance slid his arm around her. He was trying to distract her by suggesting that she now talked to Laura to make sure that there was nothing of importance to her that Gareth could take from the apartment. Maybe then they should reopen the shop, as people would undoubtedly be wondering what was going on.

Laura looked nervous. Gwyn's mother, she admitted, had once confessed to her that she believed the shop would be far safer in Gwyn's hands. While Gareth had never shared their enthusiasm, Gwyn had embraced it all. All that Laura knew was that the will that they had made out had been left with the solicitor for safekeeping. It had been as though Gwyn's parents had known that something was going to happen to them. Laura had no idea what was in the will. She had simply wanted to help Gwyn yesterday, and make sure that she received everything that had been left to her.

Mr Brookes had decided to keep a very close eye on what Gareth was actually taking from the flat, leaving his wife to make some coffee and join Gwyn, Lance and Laura in the office behind the shop. Gwyn was now showing Laura the latest set of accounts, having already shown her a copy of the will. Laura was obviously shocked, her voice barely louder than a whisper when she eventually spoke. She had often suspected that Gareth had been taking more than he should have from the shop. She had never dreamed, however, that it was on this scale. It was obvious that he had an awful lot of money, to which he had not been entitled, to pay back.

Gwyn had already insisted that Gareth reimbursed Lance's father for the embroideries. All of the rest, though... Gwyn hesitated. Right now she was not absolutely sure that she did want any of it back. She had the shop, the blueprints for the designs and, most importantly, all of her mother's tapestries back. It was far more than everything that she used to have, and she was not sure that she could live with the guilt of being as callous as her brother had been. She did not want Gareth accusing her of being heartless. And looking at the accounts, she believed that it would not take long to build up that level of profit again.

"You are staying, aren't you?" Gwyn suddenly asked Laura. "I've assumed that you will, and I have no idea what I'll do if you decide not to."

"Yes, I'll stay." Laura nodded, smiling wryly. Gareth had been in a foul mood when he had returned to the shop the previous day, and had accused his sister of performing some kind of witchcraft in order to embarrass him. Laura could not tell Gwyn what her brother had said, though, just as she couldn't tell her about the letter of resignation that was still in her bag. Gwyn and the Brookeses had arrived before she had had the chance to hand it over this morning, and now she decided to leave it where it was and burn it when she returned home at the end of the day. With Gwyn here now, Laura could sense that things were going to be completely different. She could relax as she told Gwyn how much she was looking forward to working with her.

"Oh, Gwyn's moving to Boston to be with us," Mrs Brookes announced. "Once everything is sorted out here, including taking on someone else if you believe that you need some extra help, Gwyn will be leaving. I'm sure she'll pop over regularly, though, to check that everything is all right. She wants to concentrate on designing, you see. It's all so very exciting, don't you think?"

Laura noticed that Gwyn and Lance looked at each other; yet decided to remain silent. Mrs Brookes, however, appeared oblivious. Laura decided to say nothing; instead smiling politely as she agreed that she too was looking forward to seeing how well the designs would sell in America. Mrs Brookes was talking on, still oblivious to the tension that was coming from Gwyn and Lance.

"Me and Gwyn will be coming over here over the next few days," Mrs Brookes announced, "and we'll be looking at the way the shop's run and gathering copies of the design blueprints so that we can take them over to America. Oh, I'm so looking forward to working with you all."

Laura was glad to return to the reopened shop, leaving Gwyn and Mrs Brookes looking through the paperwork. To Gwyn, it all looked so alien. She had never seen anything like this before. It was a far cry from designing and stitching. Quickly finding the blueprints for the designs, they checked them through to make sure that they were all there. Gwyn was still in a daze as she stared at it all, looking round when Lance once again slid an arm around her. He was here beside her, which was all that she needed.

Gwyn managed a half-hearted smile as she relaxed a little. She just needed time to get used to all of this. She had had no idea of the amount of work that was involved to produce the finished product. Gareth was the one who had dealt with all of that, shielding her from it as he kept her well out of the way. The initial panic was already subsiding and being replaced with a steadfast resolution to learn and understand every step of the process. She could not let Gareth beat her now.

With Gareth gone, Mr Brookes eventually rejoined them. Gareth had loaded his possessions into his car and gone. Mr Brookes had already called a locksmith and arranged for someone to come straight over. If he did try, Gareth would not be able to return. And once that was done, they could return to Bristol so that he and Lance could return to the office and continue with their own work. Lance's mother and Gwyn could come back here and get this shop sorted out. This realm was the domain of women; and was of no interest to him.

Mr Brookes drove the car back to Bristol, his wife constantly reminding him that they drove on the left in this country. With Gwyn and Lance sitting in the back, they preferred not to look. They would be separated tomorrow, and Lance would be forced to remain in Bristol with his father while Gwyn and his mother returned to Glastonbury. But the sooner the shop was sorted out, the sooner the women would not have to make that journey, and maybe then Mr and Mrs Brookes would return to Boston and leave Gwyn and Lance to settle into a routine of their own.

Gwyn headed straight to the kitchen to begin preparing dinner when they got back to the apartment. Lance followed her eagerly, switching on the kettle before slipping his arms around her waist as he stood behind her. His parents were in the living room discussing the running of the shop; inadvertently giving the pair a few precious minutes on their own. Lance did not want to be parted from Gwyn over the next few days, and he certainly did not want to spend that time with his father instead. They did not, however, appear to have any choice.

Gwyn smiled softly. She knew that the sooner they began this task, the sooner it would be done, and it was time for her to learn everything she needed to learn about the successful running of the shop. She needed to know and understand how it all worked, otherwise she might as well hand it all back to Gareth, and at least Lance's mother would now be able to realize her ambitions that much quicker. She would also be able to sell all of the designs, and not just the new ones that Gwyn had not yet had the chance to start. With Laura's help, they could make a fresh start and run the shop in the way that they wanted. There would be no more secrets. There was going to be nothing hidden away.

Lance smiled and kissed the back of her neck. He wanted the next few days to be over and his parents to return to Boston. Then they would have the apartment to themselves again. They would be left alone once more. For Lance, the next few days could not pass quickly enough.

Chapter 34

Gwyn's initial nerves over returning to the shop soon melted away, to be replaced by enjoyment at the prospect of making those trips every day for a week. It gave her the unexpected opportunity to meet up with old friends, and discover what they had been doing during her absence. With someone found to provide the extra help that Laura needed, they then sat down and discussed how they could best run the shop. With Gareth gone, the atmosphere was now relaxed and friendly.

Mrs Brookes had spent the week working tirelessly on a portfolio of every design that had been created and produced by Gwyn and her mother. Also taking notes of what people were looking for in order to provide her future daughter-in-law with some creative inspiration, she had everything that she needed ready to be packed for her journey back to Boston. Lance too had played a part, his mother dragging him away from the office so that she could charge him with the creation of a computer programme for Laura's use in the production of the designs. With a website also designed, they now had access to countless internet customers.

Soon there was nothing to keep them at the shop, and they could step back once more and leave Laura in charge. Gwyn was free to resume working on her latest design, while Mrs Brookes made countless telephone calls and website checks. Lance was free to return to the office, his father now realizing what little progress his son had made while here. An explanation was being demanded, and Lance sensed King Arthur rising up inside him as he gave him the courage, support and confidence that he now needed.

"I'm sorry, sir," Lance's voice was calm and quiet, "but I'm afraid that we've been too preoccupied with the Petersons' plan to deceive you and take everything that you've worked so hard to achieve from you. We've been concentrating on trying to work out how to prevent that from happening, and because of that, I can only apologize for falling behind with what I should have been doing. I appear to have run out of time to be able to put that right."

Blake Brookes hummed thoughtfully and said nothing. Only when back at the apartment later that evening did he make an announcement that made Lance, Gwyn and Nancy all look at him in surprise.

"I've been considering things very carefully today," he stated, "and after everything that has happened over the last year, I'm going to send you back here after your wedding, Lance, so that you can spend a second year here. You're to spend that time learning everything that you need to know about the branch here so that you'll be more use to me back at home. It'll also give Gwyn the opportunity to tie everything up and make all the final arrangements for her to move to America."

Mr Brookes was already concentrating upon the screen of the laptop. He did not notice the way that Lance and Gwyn looked at each other as he booked a flight back home for himself and his wife. At last they returned home, Lance and Gwyn taking them to the airport so that they could watch the aeroplane take off before returning to the apartment. Now they could relax again, and enjoy being in each other's company.

Two days passed before they ventured out again. There was some warmth in the wind that was blowing, while white clouds moved gracefully across the sky above them. With most people at work, the hills were relatively quiet. Another two days, and then Lance knew that he would have to return to the office. Two more blissful days before he was to spend most of the day being parted from Gwyn once more. He did not want to think about that, though, preferring to focus on the here and now, with Gwyn by his side. This was what his life was supposed to be about. This was where he really belonged.

The pair sat down on the short turf as they stared out across the open hillside. They had sat right here on so many occasions before, though now Lance had his arm around Gwyn as she leaned back against him. They had been surrounded by trees on those previous occasions, and they had gazed out across a lake towards a mist-shrouded island. Both of them could still see it – that image clearly in their minds. No-one else could, but that did not mean that it no longer existed. It would always be here, and in their hearts and minds, they both knew that.

Lance tenderly kissed the side of Gwyn's head. Sitting here, with Gwyn by his side, he knew that right here was where he truly belonged. In a few short months they would be married and finally united as one. They would then spend a month in Boston before returning here. At least his father had given him a reprieve by deciding to send him back for a second year.

Gwyn smiled as she settled back against Lance. She felt comfortable and warm while in his company, and loved every moment that she could spend with him. She did not want to think about the future while they were sitting here. She wanted to live for this moment and enjoy the present. She could think of nowhere else where she would rather be. The prospect of going to Boston, however, was nonetheless exciting. If she was going to be fair, she did have to go there so that she could see and experience the city for herself.

Guinevere and Arthur had been right. Avalon would always be with them, no matter where they were. They did not need to physically see it to be able to feel its presence. Whether they eventually decided to settle here or in Boston, Avalon would always be by their side. For them, there was no escaping. Lance smiled, a warm sensation spreading right through him as he hugged Gwyn a little more tightly. Like Arthur and Guinevere, Avalon itself would live on. Through Gwyn and Lance, their existence was now secure. Feeling close to their mystical place, Gwyn and Lance sat in silence. No-one needed to tell them what they already knew. Avalon indeed lived on.